MONSIEUR
PAMPLEMOUSSE
TAKES THE CURE

Monsieur PAMPLEMOUSSE Takes the Cure

MICHAEL BOND

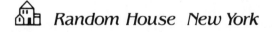 Random House New York

Bond, Michael.
  Monsieur Pamplemousse takes the cure.

  I. Title.
PR6052.052M69   1988   823'914   88–42652
ISBN 0-394-57033-2

Manufactured in the United States of America
98765432
First American Edition

Contents

MONSIEUR PAMPLEMOUSSE TAKES THE CURE

1

The Ideal Inspector

"Entrez!"

The director's voice sounded brisk and businesslike. It was undoubtedly the voice of someone who commanded and who also expected to be obeyed without question.

In the short space of time left at his disposal between rapping on the door and taking hold of the handle, Monsieur Pamplemousse tried to analyze it still further.

Was it, *par exemple,* the voice of a man who commanded and expected to be obeyed, and yet had also read his, Monsieur Pamplemousse's, recent article on the subject of *cassoulet*—its many forms and regional variations—which had recently appeared in *L'Escargot, Le Guide*'s staff magazine? And if so, was it the voice of a man who couldn't wait to hear more?

In the remaining half second or so before he turned the handle, a dry cough—an obvious clearing of the throat before getting down to business—dispelled the thought. It was scarcely the cough of a man desperately trying to conceal his excitement, but more that of someone rapidly running out of patience.

On the other hand, if the summons to the director's office

wasn't to do with the article, why had he specifically mentioned the word "Toulouse" when he rang through on the internal telephone? Toulouse, the very home of *cassoulet*. And why the note of urgency? "Drop everything, Pamplemousse," had been the order of the day. "Come to my office immediately."

Perhaps the director had a cold? That was it—a cold. There were a lot around at the moment. He must have read the previous article in the December issue—the one on garlic—its use in combating man's most common ailment.

The next remark, however, confirmed his worst suspicions. The director was not in a good mood. Testiness had crept in.

"Don't hover, whoever you are. Either come in or go away."

Monsieur Pamplemousse took a deep breath, and with all the enthusiasm of an early Christian entering the lion's den, did as he was bidden.

Having entered the room, he waited for the usual nod indicating that he could sit in the chair facing the director's desk, a desk so placed that its occupant had his back to the light and his face in the shadows—just as he, Pamplemousse, had arranged his own desk in the days when, as a member of the Sûreté, he'd wished to conduct a cross-examination in his office at the *quai des Orfèvres*.

But he waited in vain. Instead, the director gave a grunt and picked up a printed form from a neat pile in front of him. Adjusting his glasses, he gazed at it distastefully for a moment or two.

"I have been studying your medical report, Pamplemousse."

Monsieur Pamplemousse shifted uneasily. *"Oui, Monsieur le directeur?"*

"It makes unhappy reading."

Monsieur Pamplemousse felt tempted to say, if that was the case, why bother? Why not try reading something more

4

cheerful instead; his report concerning the continued insistence of French chefs on the use of fresh ingredients, for example. But wisely, he refrained. The director was clearly in no mood for frivolities. In any case he was speaking again, intoning from the form rather in the manner of a small-part actor who has been given the telephone directory to read while auditioning for the part of Hamlet.

"Born: nineteen twenty-eight.

"Height," Monsieur Pamplemousse instinctively drew himself up, "one hundred and seventy-two centimeters.

"Weight: *ninety-eight kilograms.*"

The director made it sound like a series of misprints, each a greater travesty of the truth than the one before.

"I have large bones, *Monsieur.*"

"They have need to be, Pamplemousse," said the director severely. "They are bones which may well, as they grow older, have difficulty in supporting your weight. Unless . . . steps are taken.

"Complexion: *pique-nique.* I have never heard of that before."

"It is a little-used medical term, *Monsieur.* It means pink, full of health. Even Doctor Labarre was impressed."

The director barely suppressed a snort. "Blood pressure . . ." he paused again and then held the piece of paper up to the light as if he could scarcely believe his eyes. "Blood pressure . . . can this figure be true?"

"It was not a good day, *Monsieur,* the day of the medical examination. Madame Pamplemousse was being a little difficult, you understand, and that affected me. It had been raining and Pommes Frites had the misfortune to step in something untoward while he was out for his morning walk. We had just purchased a new carpet . . ."

Monsieur Pamplemousse heard his voice trail away as the director reduced him to silence with a world-weary gesture of his hand.

"Facts, Pamplemousse. Facts are facts, and there is no

getting away from them. It is high time we returned to first principles, principles laid down by our founder, Hippolyte Duval, without whose integrity, without whose dedication, single-mindedness, clear thinking, foresight, and devotion to duty none of us would be where we are today."

While he was talking the director transferred his gaze to a large oil painting that occupied the center of the wall to his right. Lit by a single spotlight, it showed an ascetic-looking man eating alone outside a hotel on the banks of the Marne. Dressed in the fashion of the day, he gazed at the artist and the world through eyes as cold and as blue as the empty mussel shells piled high on a plate beside him. With one hand he held a glass of white wine by its stem—probably a Sancerre if the artist had accurately captured the label on the bottle. With his other hand he caressed one end of a waxed moustache, the curve of which neatly echoed the handlebars of a bicycle propped against a nearby tree. It was one of many velocipedes dotted about the picture, for the motor car had yet to be invented. *Le Guide* itself was still in its infancy, confining its investigations to those restaurants in and around Paris that could be reached by Monsieur Duval on two wheels or by pony and trap.

While agreeing with the director that but for Hippolyte Duval he wouldn't be standing where he was, Monsieur Pamplemousse couldn't help but reflect that, given the present circumstances, the advantages this implied were open to debate. He'd always nursed a secret feeling that had he and the founder of *Le Guide* ever met they wouldn't necessarily have seen eye to eye. He suspected Monsieur Duval lacked humor. The faint smile on his face looked out of place, rather as if it had been hired specially for the occasion. Either that, or he had just witnessed one of his fellow cyclists falling from his machine.

The director's next words confirmed this feeling. Reaching into a drawer in his desk he took out a plastic box, opened it, and withdrew a small red object, which he held up for Monsieur Pamplemousse to see.

"In his later years," he said, "our founder made a great study of the effect too much food can have on the body. He came to the conclusion that man can live happily on an apple a day. A dictum, Aristide, which, if I may say so, you would do well to consider."

As the crunch that punctuated this last statement died away, Monsieur Pamplemousse gazed at the director with something approaching horror. It was a well-known fact that people often grew to look like their pets—he had himself been compared more than once to Pommes Frites, but that was different, a compliment of the highest order. It was the first time he'd encountered someone who had grown to look like another person's portrait. It hadn't occurred to him until now, but there was no denying the fact that the director bore a distinct resemblance to the erstwhile incumbent of his post, Monsieur Hippolyte Duval himself. There was the same fanatical gleam in his eyes, a gleam which brooked no interference or disagreement.

"With the greatest respect, *Monsieur,*" he said at last, "I would not call making do with an apple a day *living*—nor would I connect it with the word *happiness.* I also feel most strongly that it is a philosophy which ill becomes a man whose whole life was dedicated to the running of a restaurant guide. Speaking personally, I would find it impossible to conduct my work for *Le Guide* were I to confine myself to such a diet. An inspector has to sample, to test. He has to compare and evaluate. Above all, he has to accumulate experience, experience that embraces both the good and the bad. There are times when he has to consume meals when all his natural instincts tell him to stop. People think it is easy. The few—the very few—who know how I earn my living, say to me 'Pamplemousse, how lucky you are. How wonderful to have such a job.' But if they only knew.

"Were I to confine myself to an apple a day, why . . ."
Monsieur Pamplemousse gazed out of the window as he
sought hard to find a suitable parallel and ended up on the
banks of the Seine somewhere near the *quai des Orfèvres*.
"Why it would be like an inspector of the Sûreté patting a
murderer on the head and saying, 'Go away and don't ever
let me catch you doing that again.' It would make a mockery
of my calling.

"Being a little overweight goes hand in hand with my
work, *Monsieur*. It is an occupational hazard—a cross we
inspectors have to bear, along with occasional bouts of indigestion alone in our beds at night."

"Yes, yes, Pamplemousse." The director interrupted in
a tone of voice that all too clearly meant "No! No!"

Rifling through some papers on his desk he extracted
another sheet. Monsieur Pamplemousse's heart sank as he
recognized the familiar buff color of a form P39. It had a
red star attached to it. It was the one Madame Grante in
Accounts used when a decision from higher authority was
needed.

"I have been going through your expenses, Pamplemousse. They, too, make unhappy reading. Unless, of
course, we happened to be thinking of applying to the
Gulbenkian Foundation for a grant. In those circumstances
they would provide welcome evidence of the mounting cost
of our operation.

"If you are so concerned about the state of your digestion, I suggest the occasional bottle of *eau minérale* instead
of wine would not come amiss.

"On the tenth of January, for example, you and Pommes
Frites between you consumed an entire bottle of Château
Lafite with your *boeuf bourguignon*. Considering the remarks
you made in your report concerning lapses in the *cuisine*—
I see you compared the quality of the meat with a certain
brand of shoe leather—might not a wine from a lesser

8

château have sufficed? Perhaps even a *pichet* of the house red?"

"If you were to check with my P41, *Monsieur,* you would see that January the tenth was my birthday. Rennes is not the most exciting place in which to spend one's birthday—especially in mid-January. And it was raining . . ."

"Be that as it may, Pamplemousse, there is no getting away from the fact that you are grossly overweight and it is high time something was done about it." The director gestured toward the far side of the room. "Stand over there, please, and look at yourself in the mirror."

As Monsieur Pamplemousse turned he gave a start. In the corner behind the door stood another figure. For a brief moment he thought a third person had been a party to their conversation, and he was about to express his indignation in no uncertain terms when something about its posture made him pause. It was a dummy, an exceptionally lifelike one, complete in every detail down to the very last button on its jacket, but a dummy nevertheless.

"Allow me to introduce our latest recruit, Pamplemousse." The director sounded pleased at the effect he had achieved. "His name is Alphonse. No doubt you are wondering why he is there?"

Glad to be able to divert the conversation away from his P39, Monsieur Pamplemousse murmured his agreement. Expenses were always a thorny subject and it was no easy matter to strike a happy balance between the need to eat at some of the most expensive restaurants in France while at the same time not to overstep the rigid boundaries laid down by an ever vigilant Madame Grante, many of whose minions were hard put to eat out at a local *bistro* more than twice a week.

The director rose to his feet. "Alphonse, Pamplemousse, represents the *Ideal Inspector.* An ideal we must all of us strive for in the future. I have been studying the man

9

writings of our founder and the results have been fed into a computer. From its findings I have had this model constructed.

"I think," the director formed a steeple with his hands and tapped the end of his nose reflectively as he began to pace the room, "I think I can say without fear of contradiction, that I know his background and his habits as well as I know my own.

"I know where he was born; where he went to school. I know where he lives. I know the number of rooms in his apartment and how they are furnished, what time he goes to bed, when he rises. I know his tastes and where he buys his clothes. I know where he goes for his holidays. In short, I know down to the very last detail what makes him tick.

"The ideal inspector working for *Le Guide,* Pamplemousse, will weigh seventy-six point eight kilos. He will lead an active life, rising at six-thirty every morning and taking a cold shower. In his leisure hours he will play tennis, perhaps a little squash from time to time—enough to keep his figure in trim. During his lifetime he will have no more than two point six mistresses—"

Monsieur Pamplemousse, who had been growing steadily more depressed as he listened to the growing list of what he could only interpret as his own deficiencies, could stand it no longer.

"With respect, *Monsieur,*" he exclaimed, eyeing Alphonse distastefully, "it is hard to imagine him having point six of a mistress, let alone any more."

"Would that we could all say that, Pamplemousse," said the director severely. "Two point six would be a very low estimate indeed for some of us. That unfortunate business with the girls from the Follies, the reason for your early retirement from the Sûreté—that should keep you ahead of the national average for many years to come."

Monsieur Pamplemousse fell silent. When the director

had a bee in his bonnet it was pointless to argue, and on this occasion he was clearly dealing with not one bee, but a veritable swarm. He braced himself mentally for the next blow, wondering just how and where it would land.

"I must say, Pamplemousse," continued the director, "that in many respects you fall sadly short of the ideal. In fairness, I have to admit you are not alone in this. Looking at the group photograph taken during the staff outing at Boulogne last year, clearly many of your colleagues would fare equally badly were they to stand alongside our friend here, but their turn will come. However, for reasons which I won't go into for the moment, it is you whom we have selected for the honor of acting as a guinea pig for what we have in mind.

"For some time now the Board of Governors has been considering various ways in which we might expand our activities—broaden our horizons as it were. In many respects it goes against the grain, but one has to move with the times and there is no denying that some of our competitors have been forced into taking similar action. Michelin ventured into other countries many years ago. Gault-Millau currently involve themselves in areas that would make our founder turn in his grave were he to be aware of them—magazines, special offers, things I trust we shall never do.

"Nevertheless, it is our intention from time to time to test other waters, if I may coin a phrase. And first on the list is a survey of all the health farms in France.

"Pamplemousse, tomorrow we want you to dip our toes into the waters of the Pyrénées-Orientales. A room is reserved for you at an establishment north of Perpignan. I wish you luck and I look forward to welcoming the new Pamplemousse on his return in a fortnight's time."

Having delivered himself of this salvo, a positive broadside of unexpected facts, the director came to a halt opposite Monsieur Pamplemousse, all ammunition spent, and held out his hand.

"Bon voyage, Aristide," he said, eyeing the other some-what nervously.

"A fortnight!" Monsieur Pamplemousse repeated the words with all the disbelief and bitterness he could muster. "At a *health farm!* Has *Monsieur* ever *been* to the Pyrénées-Orientales in March? All the winter snow will be beginning to melt. It will be cascading down the mountainside in ice-cold torrents. It is not *our* toes that will suffer, *Monsieur,* it is *mine.* I hate to think what might happen to them were I to risk dipping them into such waters. At the very least they will become frostbitten. At worst, gangrene could set in and before you know where you are, *pouf!* They will fall off!"

"Come, come, Aristide, you mustn't take me too liter-ally." The director stole a quick glance at his watch as he motioned Monsieur Pamplemousse toward the visitor's chair. As he feared, it was almost lunch time. It was all taking much longer than he'd planned. A good man, Pam-plemousse, but not one to be hurried. Information had to be digested and slept on. A typical Capricorn, and from the Auvergne as well—a difficult combination; whereas the new model—the *Ideal* Inspector—he was definitely a Leo and from some less mountainous region.

"Dipping our toes was perhaps an unhappy turn of phrase, but don't you think, Aristide, the change will do you good?"

From the depths of the armchair Monsieur Pam-plemousse listened like a man who was experiencing a bad dream. A man whose feet became more leaden the harder he tried to escape. He sat up as a thought struck him.

"I have just remembered, *Monsieur,* it will not be possi-ble. My car is due for its two hundred thousand kilometer service. Later in the year, perhaps, when it is warmer."

"Excellent news!" The director rubbed his hands to-gether with a pleasure which was so obviously false that he had the grace to look embarrassed. "It can be done while you are away," he said hurriedly. "I will make all the necessary arrangements. After two weeks at the Château Morgue you will be in no fit state to drive anyway. The good Herr Schmuck and his wife will see to that."

Sensing that he had inadvertently struck a wrong note, the director hastily crossed to a filing cabinet and withdrew a green folder. Opening it up, he spread the contents across his desk. Recognizing the detachable pages contained at the back of every copy of *Le Guide,* the ones on which readers were invited to make their own comments, Monsieur Pamplemousse wondered what was going to happen next.

"It doesn't sound so bad. Preliminary investigations have already been taking place." The director sifted through the papers and after a moment or two found what he had been looking for. "Look, here is one taken at random. I will read it to you: 'Just like a home from home. The food was plain but wholesome, avoiding the excessive use of cream common to so many establishments. The first time we encountered genuine smiles in all our travels through France. My wife and I particularly enjoyed the early morning tramps through the snow (obligatory without a medical certificate). Our only criticism concerned the beds, which could have been softer, and the lack of pillows. It would also help if the bicycle racks were provided with locks. In many ways it reminded us both of our days in the Forces (my wife was an AT).' "

"An *at!*" repeated Monsieur Pamplemousse. "What is an *at?*"

The director ran a hand round his collar and then glanced at the window, wondering if he should open it. The room was getting warm. "It was some kind of paramilitary female organization operating from *Grande Bretagne* during the war." He tried to sound as casual as possible.

"You mean the people who wrote that report were *English?*" exclaimed Monsieur Pamplemousse.

It figured. Memories of a week he'd once spent in Torquay during a particularly cold winter just after the war came flooding back to him. It had been his first visit to England and at the time he'd sworn it would be his last. An unheated bedroom. Everyone speaking in whispers at breakfast lest they incur the wrath of the landlady, a bizarre creature of uncertain temper who spoke some totally incomprehensible language and who wouldn't let anyone back inside her house until after five-thirty in the afternoon. A depressing experience. Fourteen meals of soggy fish and chips—eaten out of a newspaper! He'd spent most of his time sitting in a shelter on the sea front trying to decipher the crossword.

"It suffers a little in translation," began the director.

"May I see the others, *Monsieur*? The *less* random ones?"

"They vary." The director began to gather them up. "Some, perhaps, are not quite so enthusiastic."

"S'il vous plaît, Monsieur."

The director sighed. It had been worth a try.

"Not quite so favorable!" Monsieur Pamplemousse could scarcely conceal his scorn as he glanced through the pile of reports. *"Sacré bleu!* They are like an overripe Camembert—they stink! I have never seen such reports, *never*. Not in the whole of my career. Look at them.

" 'The man should be arrested . . . his wife, too . . . Herr Schmuck is a . . .' "

There the report ended in a series of blots, rather as though the emotional strain of putting pen to paper had proved so great the author had emptied the entire contents of an ink-well over the report rather than commit blasphemy in writing.

"That settles it!" He rose to his feet. "I am sorry, *Monsieur*."

The director heaved another sigh, a deeper one this time. "I am sorry too, Aristide. I had hoped that your dedication to duty, the dedication we older hands at *Le Guide* have come to admire and respect, would have been sufficient motivation. Alas . . ." With an air of one whose last illusion about his fellow man has just been irretrievably shattered, he played his trump card. "It leaves me with no alternative but to exercise the authority of my position. An authority, Pamplemousse, which I must remind you—although speaking, I hope, as a friend, it saddens me that I should have to do so—you were only too happy to accept when you first joined us. You will be leaving for Perpignan on the seven forty-one train tomorrow morning. Your tickets are with Madame Grante."

Monsieur Pamplemousse sank back into his chair again. He knew when he was beaten. What the director had just said was true. He owed *Le Guide* a great deal. The memory of that fatal day when, out of a sense of moral duty and against the advice of many of his colleagues, he had handed in his resignation at the Sûreté, was still very clear in his mind: the sudden cold feeling of being alone in the world when he'd walked out of the *quai des Orfèvres* for the last time, not knowing which way to turn—left or right. As it turned out, the Fates had been kind. Obeying a momentary impulse, he'd turned right and headed toward the seventh *arrondissement*. And as luck would have it, his wanderings had taken him past the offices of *Le Guide*. There he had bumped into the director; a director who had cause to be grateful for the satisfactory conclusion to a case which, had it been handled differently, could have brought scandal on France's oldest and most respected gastronomic bible.

But if the director had cause to be grateful to Monsieur Pamplemousse, the reverse was certainly true. Hearing of the latter's plight, he had, without a second's hesitation, offered him a job on the spot. In the space of less than an hour, Monsieur Pamplemousse had moved from one office to another, from a job he had come to think of as his life's blood, to one which was equally rewarding.

He rose to his feet. It had been a generous act, a noble act. A gesture of friendship he could never hope to repay.

He was left with no option but to accede to the director's wishes. To argue would be both churlish and unappreciative of his good fortune.

"Come, come, Aristide," the director allowed himself the luxury of putting an arm on Monsieur Pamplemousse's shoulder as he pointed him in the direction of the door. "It is only for two weeks. Two weeks out of your life. It will all be over before you know where you are."

While he was talking the director reached into an inner pocket of his jacket with his other hand and withdrew a long, white envelope. "These are a few notes which may help you in your task. There's no need to read them now. I suggest you put them away and don't look at them until you reach your destination. What is the saying? *La corde ne peut être toujours tendue.* All work and no play makes Jacques a dull boy? Who knows, they may help you to kill two *oiseaux* with one stone."

Monsieur Pamplemousse blinked. For a moment he was mentally knocked off balance by the director's disconcerting habit of mixing his languages as well as his metaphors when the occasion demanded. Absentmindedly he slipped the envelope inside his jacket without so much as a second glance.

"Oh, and another thing." As they reached the door the director paused with one hand on the latch. "I think you should take Pommes Frites with you. He, too, has been looking overweight in recent weeks. I think he is still suffering from your visit to Les Cinq Parfaits. Besides, you may find him of help in your activities."

Monsieur Pamplemousse's spirits sank still further. It hadn't occurred to him for one moment that he might not be taking Pommes Frites. Pommes Frites always went with him. He was glad he hadn't thought of the possibility earlier, otherwise he might have said more than he had already and regretted it.

"Dogs are not normally allowed at *Établissements Ther-*

maux," said the director, reading his thoughts, "not even with the payment of a supplement. It is a question of *hygiène*. Not," he raised his hands in mock horror at the thought, "not that one questions Pommes Frites's personal habits for one moment. But the presence of dogs seems to be particularly frowned on at Château Morgue. *Chiens* are definitely not catered for. I had to resort to a subterfuge. I insisted on his presence on account of your unfortunate disability."

"My disability, *Monsieur?*"

The director clucked impatiently. Pamplemousse was being unusually difficult this morning. Difficult, or deliberately unhelpful; he strongly suspected the latter.

"The trouble with your sight. I made a telephone call on your behalf late yesterday evening in order to explain the situation. I'm sure Pommes Frites will make an excellent guide dog. It's the kind of thing bloodhounds ought to be good at. You can collect his special harness along with some dark glasses and a white stick at the same time as the tickets."

Monsieur Pamplemousse stared at the director as if he had suddenly taken leave of his senses. "Perhaps, *Monsieur,"* he exclaimed, "you would like me to learn Braille on the journey down?"

His sarcasm fell on deaf ears. "Such dedication, Aristide! I knew from the outset you were the right man for the job."

"But . . ." Monsieur Pamplemousse found himself clutching at straws, straws which were wrenched from his hand the moment his grip tightened. 'Would it not be easier and infinitely more satisfactory if someone else went?"

"Easier, Pamplemousse, *oui."* The director's voice cut across his own like a pistol shot. "More satisfactory . . . *non!* We need someone with your knowledge and experience, receptive to new ideas, able to collect and collate information. Someone totally incorruptible.

"Oh, and one final thing," the director's voice, softer now, reached Monsieur Pamplemousse as if through a haze.

"I am assuming that to all intents and purposes your *régime* has already begun. There is, I believe, a restaurant car on the *Morning Capitole*. However, I shall not expect to see any items from its menu appear on your expense sheet. It will be good practice for you and Pommes Frites, and it will put you both in the right frame of mind for all the optional extras at Château Morgue—such things as massages and needle baths. Make full use of everything. Do not stint yourselves. I will see things right with Madame Grante.

"And now," the director held out his hand, donning his official manner at the same time, *"au revoir,* Aristide, and . . . *bonne chance."*

Although the handshake was not without warmth, the message that went with it was icily clear, delivered in the manner of one who has said all there is to say on the subject and now wishes to call the meeting closed.

The director believed in running *Le Guide* with all the efficiency of a military operation, and clearly in his mind's eye Monsieur Pamplemousse was already but a flag on the map of France that occupied one entire wall of the Operations Room in the basement; a magnetic flag which on the morrow would be moved steadily but inexorably southward as the *Morning Capitole* gathered speed and headed toward Toulouse and the Pyrénées-Orientales.

As Monsieur Pamplemousse made his way slowly back down the corridor toward the lift, he turned a corner and collided with a girl coming the other way. She was carrying a large tray on which reposed an earthenware pot, a plate, bread, cutlery, napkin, and a bottle of wine: a Pommard '72.

"Zut!" The girl neatly recovered her balance and then made great play of raising the tray in triumph as she recognized Monsieur Pamplemousse. *"Alors!* That was a near thing. *Monsieur le directeur* would not have been pleased if his *cassoulet* had gone all over the floor. Nor would the chef

—he made it specially. *Monsieur le directeur* said to me when he phoned down a moment ago how much he was looking forward to it. I think he has had a bad morning."

"Cassoulet!" Monsieur Pamplemousse repeated the word bitterly as the girl hurried on her way. *"Cassoulet!"* He had a sudden mental picture of the director clutching his apple sanctimoniously while he laid down the law. The mockery of it all! The hypocrisy!

He hesitated for a moment, wondering whether he should snatch a quick bite to eat before visiting Madame Grante, and decided against it. His digestive tracts were in a parlous enough state as it was without adding to their problems.

Besides, if he was to catch the early morning train there was work to be done. His desk would need to be cleared of outstanding papers, the contents of *Le Guide*'s issue suitcase would have to be checked. He had a feeling some of the items might come in very useful over the next two weeks—the portable cooking equipment for a start.

The thought triggered off another. He might try and persuade old Rabiller in Stores to let him borrow a remote control attachment for his Leica while he was away. He'd heard there was one in stock awaiting field trials. With time on his hands he might try his hand at some wildlife photography. An eagle's nest, perhaps? Or a mountain bear stirring after its long winter rest. He would take the precaution of stocking up on film.

Then he would need to be home early in order to break the news to Madame Pamplemousse. She would not be pleased. He had promised faithfully to decorate the kitchen before the spring. That would have to wait now, and in his weakened state after "the cure" who knew when he might be fit enough to start work on it?

Pommes Frites, too. Pommes Frites liked his set routine. They would need to be on their way by half past six at the very latest, which would mean doing him out of his morning walk. There was also the little matter of getting him used to his new harness before they set out.

Almost imperceptibly Monsieur Pamplemousse quickened his pace. One way and another there was a lot to be done and very little time left in which to do it.

2

The Doppelgänger

With his suitcase stowed away in the compartment at the
end of the carriage, his overcoat and white stick on the
luggage rack above his head, Monsieur Pamplemousse
removed his dark glasses, gathered the little that was left of
his breath, and gazed gloomily out of the window of the
Morning Capitole as it slid gently out of the deserted *quais*
of the Gare d'Austerlitz and then rapidly gathered speed.
   The day had got off to a bad start. Trouble had set in
almost as soon as they left home, a fact which Pommes
Frites, already curled up on the floor as he addressed himself to the task of catching up on some lost sleep, would
have been only too happy to confirm had he been asked.
   Any fond hopes Monsieur Pamplemousse might have
cherished about his "condition" conferring little extra
privileges *en route* had been quickly dashed. The cup containing the milk of human kindness ran dry very early in the
day on the Paris *Métro,* as he discovered when he tried to
board an already crowded train at Lamarck-Caulaincourt.
The *"poufs"* and snorts and cluckings which rose from all
sides as he attempted to push his way through to the seats
normally reserved for *les mutilés de guerre, les femmes enceintes*

and other deserving travelers in descending order of priority, had to be heard to be believed. In no time at all he found himself back on the platform, glasses askew and suitcase threatening to burst at the seams. Had he not managed to get in some quick and effective jabs with his stick, Pommes Frites might well have suffered a bruised tail—or worse—as the doors slid shut behind them and the train went on its way.

Seeing him standing there and misinterpreting the reason, a more helpful morning commuter who arrived on the platform just in time to see them alight, came to the rescue and escorted him back to the waiting lift. Monsieur Pamplemousse was too kindly a person to throw this act of friendship back into the face of his unknown benefactor, so he allowed himself to be ushered into the lift, hearing as he did so the arrival and departure of the next train.

Then, on emerging at the top, he'd collided with an ex-colleague from the Sûreté. The look on the man's face as he caught Monsieur Pamplemousse in the act of removing his dark glasses in order to get his bearings, plainly mirrored his embarrassment and contempt. The news would be round all the stations by now, probably even the *quai des Orfèvres* itself. "Old Pamplemousse has really hit rock bottom. He's trying the 'blind man on the *Métro*' routine now. Things must be bad. First the Follies and now this. No doubt about it, an *oeuf mauvais.*"

The prospect through the window as he took his seat on the *Morning Capitole* was gray. The Seine, from the few glimpses he managed to catch, looked dark and uninviting. Ahead of them lights from anonymous office blocks twinkled through the mist, beckoning to the trickle of early arrivals hurrying to beat the morning rush.

Suddenly, as the Seine joined up with the Marne and then disappeared from view, he felt glad to be heading south and away from it all. He was conscious of a warm glow that owed as much to the thought of going somewhere fresh as it did to the unaccustomed flurry of exercise. It was a feeling that was almost immediately enhanced by an announcement over the loudspeakers that breakfast was about to be served. To the devil with the director and his instructions!

Giving Pommes Frites a warning nudge, he rose to his feet. If the other passengers on the train felt as he did there would be a rush for tables.

If only Ananas had not been on the same train; worse still, he occupied the same carriage. That was the unkindest cut of all—really rubbing salt into the wound, the kind of bizarre coincidence he could well have done without. Experience in the Force had taught him that most people have a double somewhere in the world, but more often than not their paths never cross, or if they do, they pass each other by in the street without recognizing the fact, aware only of experiencing something slightly odd—a feeling of *déjà vu*.

It was his particular misfortune to have a double whose face was constantly in the public eye, made larger than life by being plastered on billboards the length and breadth of France, and consequently in Monsieur Pamplemousse's opinion—despite the element of self-criticism it implied—made ten times less inviting.

As he led the way along the corridor toward the restaurant car, he glanced into the compartment where Ananas was holding court. Adopting a pose which ensured that his profile was clearly visible to anyone passing, he was deep in conversation with a somewhat vicious-looking individual. Monsieur Pamplemousse reflected that Ananas's companion looked as if he might have even stranger proclivities than his master, which would be saying something.

If Ananas recognized himself in Monsieur Pamplemousse he showed no sign, but then he probably didn't encounter the same problems. On occasion even the simple act of eating in a restaurant became something of a bore, with its

23

routine of pretended mistaken identity, while other diners tried to make up their minds whether or not they were in the presence of the real thing.

Croissants, toast, *confiture,* and *café* arrived with lightning speed, and by the time they were passing through Brétigny he was sipping a glass of *jus d'orange* and feeling better. He wondered idly where Ananas might be going at this time of the year. Perhaps his television program was having a break. He was too sharp an operator and had too much at stake to let someone else take over while he was away. For all their present loyalty, the public were a fickle lot and he would be well aware of the double risk of having either a stand-in who was more popular than himself or someone a great deal less so. Either way he could stand to lose.

Ananas had first appeared on the scene some years before as "Oncle Hubert" on a children's television program. "Oncle Hubert" had a "way" with children. Particularly, as things turned out, with little girls.

Monsieur Pamplemousse could have told his many fan clubs a thing or two. There had been a near scandal which, in the less liberal climate of the time, would have meant the end of his career had it ever come to light. As it was, strings must have been pulled by someone on high, for "Oncle Hubert" had conveniently disappeared for a while, ostensibly suffering from nervous exhaustion due to overwork.

When he resurfaced under his adopted name, it was as host of a particularly infantile afternoon game show, which by some quirk of fate caught the public's imagination. In a relatively short space of time the viewing figures rocketed to the top, carrying Ananas with them and the accolade of a prime spot two evenings a week. From that moment on he had never looked back. Almost overnight he became that strange product of the twentieth century—a "television personality"—whose views on matters of moment were sought and listened to with awe. Without doubt, Ananas would be careful not to court disaster again.

At 8:25 they reached the start of the twenty kilometers or so of concrete monorail north of Orleans—test-bed for an Aerotrain that never was. By then the sun had broken through and Pamplemousse's mood was lifting. Even the sight of Ananas at a table further down the restaurant car didn't dampen his spirits. Like royalty, Ananas never soiled his hands with money, even when the need arose—which wasn't often, so the bill was being paid by his companion. A good deal of his income came from payments in kind. He was careful to endorse only those products which would enrich his own life—shoes, shirts, suits, the furnishings of his several houses; all were of the very best. Cars met him wherever he went, doors opened at his approach. The story was told that when he did pay for something by check it was seldom cashed, the recipient preferring to have it framed as a souvenir, hoping it would increase in value in the fullness of time.

Settling back preparatory to paying his own bill, Monsieur Pamplemousse reached down and fondled Pommes Frites's head. He received an immediate response in the form of a luxurious and long drawn out stretching of the legs and body. It started at the tips of the forepaws and ended up some moments later at the tail. Pommes Frites liked traveling by train; there was far more room than in his master's car, and it wasn't subject to sudden and unexpected swervings, nor bouts of thumping on the steering wheel by the driver. At least, he hadn't heard any so far. He was also badly in need of reassurance, and reassurance had been very thin on the ground so far that morning.

The fact of the matter was, Pommes Frites felt in a state of utter confusion. He didn't know for sure whether he was coming or going. Or, to put it another way, he knew he was going *somewhere,* but he had no idea where or for what reason.

Normally it wouldn't have troubled him. Normally he looked forward to journeys with his master and he didn't

25

really mind where they went, but the present trip seemed different. Ever since Monsieur Pamplemousse arrived home the previous afternoon he had been acting very strangely. First of all there had been the business with the glasses. No sooner had he got indoors and taken his shoes off, than he'd put on some dark glasses, darker, much darker than the ones he sometimes wore when he was driving his car, so dark you couldn't even see his eyes. Then he'd started groping his way around the apartment as if he couldn't see where he was going—which wasn't surprising in the circumstances. Madame Pamplemousse hadn't been at all pleased when he'd knocked over a vase full of flowers, particularly when they landed on the same patch of carpet he, Pommes Frites, had been in trouble over only a few days before.

But things hadn't ended there. There was also the strange contraption he'd been made to wear. At first he'd thought it was meant for carrying the shopping, something he wouldn't have minded doing at all. Pommes Frites liked shopping and he always accompanied his master on his visits to the local market. But no, it was obviously meant to serve some other purpose. What purpose he wasn't sure as yet, except that it had to do with crossing roads. Or rather, *not* crossing roads.

That was another thing. Normally, Monsieur Pamplemousse took charge when there was any traffic about and Pommes Frites happily followed on behind, secure in the knowledge that if he stuck close to his master's heels no harm would come to him.

Now his master had taken to hovering, holding on to the new collar and tapping the edge of the pavement with a stick—almost as though he was afraid to venture any further for fear of being knocked down. They had only been out once, but in Pommes Frites's view, once was more than enough. He'd been glad to get back home again in one piece. One way and another his confidence had been badly sapped.

Last, but by no means least, there had been the encounter with the second Monsieur Pamplemousse, the one he'd caught a brief glimpse of when they boarded the train. True, on closer inspection the new one was quite different from the version he had known and loved for a number of years. One quick sniff had established that straight away. But outwardly the likeness had been remarkable: the same figure, the same way of walking, the same face, even down to a similar though not so dark pair of glasses.

It was all very confusing and for the time being at least, totally beyond his comprehension. That being so, he had given up thinking about it. Pommes Frites belonged to the school of thought that believed if you waited long enough problems had a habit of solving themselves, and it was pointless losing too much sleep over them.

All the same, he was glad to feel the touch of his master's hand. It signified that at long last things were returning to normal, and he felt in a much better frame of mind as he followed Monsieur Pamplemousse out of the restaurant car, so much so he scarcely gave the ersatz edition a second glance when they passed his table.

Back in the compartment, Pommes Frites gave the scenery a cursory inspection through the window and then resumed his nap, while his master buried himself behind a *journal.*

Châteauroux and Limoges came and went unremarked, and as they drew out of Brive-la-Gaillarde, Monsieur Pamplemousse, satisfactorily up to date on current happenings in the world at large, rose and made his way toward the dining car again in order to investigate the possibility of an early *déjeuner.* He quickly shelved the idea. Ananas was already ensconced at a table, holding forth loudly on the subject of some *coquilles St. Jacques* which were apparently not to his liking. He was giving the waiter a dressing down in no uncertain terms, much to the obvious embarrassment of the other diners. Monsieur Pamplemousse reflected wryly on the aptness of the choice of dishes, for was not Saint Jacques the patron saint of money-makers? The episode left a nasty taste in his mouth and quite put him off the thought of eating. He felt relieved he hadn't woken Pommes Frites; his change of plan would have been hard to explain. It took a lot to put Pommes Frites off his food.

By Cahors hunger pangs had started to set in, and he was beginning to regret his decision. It wasn't until 13:14 precisely, as they entered the station at Toulouse, that there occurred one of those rare events which break through the thickest cloud and cause the sun to shine, restoring at one and the same time one's faith in the world.

As they drew to a halt they were assailed on all sides by the sound of cheering. Somewhere toward the front of the train a band was playing martial music, and as he went to open the door at the end of the carriage he caught sight of a group of men waving a large banner.

Toulouse, for whatever reason, seemed to be *en fête,* and the arrival of the *Morning Capitole* was obviously the high spot of the day.

Reacting rather faster than his fellow passengers, Ananas took in the situation at a glance and pushed his way past, waving to the crowds as he went. Donning his sunglasses in order to pay lip service to the pretense of traveling incognito, he paused momentarily to adjust his composure, and then emerged in order to greet his admirers.

The effect was magical. A great cheer went up from the waiting throng as they recognized him and word went round. A moment later he disappeared from view, swallowed up in a sea of admirers, only to reappear again seconds later as he was lifted shoulder high. It struck Monsieur Pamplemousse that his smile looked somewhat fixed, as though the reception was exceeding anything even he had anticipated.

For a brief moment Monsieur Pamplemousse felt almost sorry for him. He wondered if it was like that wherever he went. In his time he'd had his own share of public attention, but it had always been a thing of the moment, a brief period of glory when he'd been responsible for solving a particularly juicy *cause célèbre*. The day after it was usually forgotten, overtaken by other events. Nowadays he was all too grateful for the strict anonymity that his work for *Le Guide* imposed. Never to be able to go anywhere without such goings-on must be dreadful.

Shortly afterward Ananas's *aide de camp* appeared, struggling beneath a large assortment of monogrammed luggage. He didn't look best pleased.

Monsieur Pamplemousse began gathering together his own belongings. At least the platform was now clear. He glanced at his watch. They had plenty of time to catch the connection to Perpignan.

Climbing down onto the platform he paused to have a brief word with the attendant.

"Au revoir. Merci." He pressed a small offering into the man's hand. It disappeared with all the professional skill of one who earned a good proportion of his living by such sleight of hand. But it was worth it. Realizing that Pommes Frites was sharing the breakfast, the man had been more than generous with the portions.

"Merci, M'sieur." The attendant was looking very pleased about something. After the unpleasantness with Ananas over *déjeuner,* Monsieur Pamplemousse couldn't believe he was deriving satisfaction from the latter's reception.

"Do you believe in justice, *M'sieur?*"

Monsieur Pamplemousse shrugged. "Most of the time. Although I must admit to a certain wavering when I witness the kind of demonstration that has just taken place."

The attendant laughed. "That is what is known as 'rough

justice,' *m'sieur*. It may get even rougher when both sides find out their mistake. It is not a demonstration of love. It is a *manifestation. Une grève sauvage,* a wildcat strike. It is over a matter of schedules. We are the last train they are allowing in today.

"I think it is one product Monsieur Ananas may regret endorsing—especially when his picture appears in the newspapers tomorrow. It could well lose him his free life pass on S.N.C.F."

He turned and looked at Monsieur Pamplemousse with some concern. *"M'sieur* is traveling far?"

Monsieur Pamplemousse nodded. "We hoped to reach Perpignan."

"In that case you should hurry. The train will be coming into *quai trois.* They are allowing the connection out because the driver lives in Narbonne, but who knows? They may yet change their minds. It may not take you on to Perpignan, but it will be a start."

Monsieur Pamplemousse thanked him and hurried down the steps and up the other side to where a train from Bordeaux had just arrived at the adjoining *quai.*

He paused as the attendant's voice called over to him. *"M'sieur."*

"Oui?"

"Forgive my saying so, but has anyone ever told you . . ."

"Oui," said Monsieur Pamplemousse. "Many times."

The attendant shrugged. *"Tant pis. C'est la vie."*

"C'est la vie!" The man was right—it was no use minding. He climbed into the waiting *Corail.* After the *Capitole* it felt like boarding an airplane. He almost expected to be told to fasten his seat belt.

The cheers from the other end of the platform had grown more sporadic; he could detect a note of disillusion. Perhaps Ananas was trying to pour oil on troubled waters while protecting his own position at the same time. He didn't envy him the task.

30

As the train moved out of the *gare* he caught a glimpse of Ananas's factotum sitting glumly on a pile of luggage. Perhaps they, too, had been hoping to make the connection. If so, they were out of luck.

He settled back to enjoy the rest of the journey, however far it took them. It had been a strange interlude, not without its compensations. Somehow it redressed the balance slightly and made up for all the little indignities he had suffered. He would enjoy relating the tale at the next year's staff outing.

He was still working it over in his mind—honing the edges as it were—when they reached Carcassonne, looking very benign as it basked in the afternoon sun, the somber history of the old town buried in shadow. The platform was deserted. In a few months' time it would be laden with produce from the surrounding countryside.

Soon they were passing through vineyards. Thirty minutes later hills ahead of them heralded Narbonne, and at Narbonne the attendant's forecast came true. There would be no more trains that day. Passengers would have to make their own arrangements.

As he joined the throng of disgruntled fellow travelers pushing their way along the subway toward the exit, Monsieur Pamplemousse decided it might be a good moment to give his accessories another airing. Perhaps the good people of Narbonne would be more sympathetic to his plight than they had been in Paris. He had happy memories of his last visit, when he'd dined at a delightful little restaurant where they played a tape of the Hallelujah Chorus to herald the arrival of the dessert "chariot." He glanced at his watch. The restaurant was due for another test and it might not be too late.

Leaving Pommes Frites in charge of the luggage trolley, he took hold of his white stick, had a quick look around in order to get his bearings, then donned the dark glasses.

Blackness descended, and once again he felt the awful

hopelessness being struck blind must engender. Heaven alone knew where the director had found them. Perhaps Madame Grante had produced them—getting her own back for some of his expense accounts. As he groped his way along the outside of the *gare* he decided that another time—not that there would ever be another time if he had any say in the matter, but *if* there were—he would insist on attending some kind of training course first.

Screwing his eyes around he spied the OFFICE DE TOU-RISME through the side of the frames. It was closed.

On the far side of the forecourt there was a large sign marked TAXIS but the area in front of it was empty. In fact taxis were conspicuous by their absence. They must all have been taken by the fleet of foot and were probably heading for destinations many kilometers away by now.

His heart sank and he was about to give up when he heard a voice. Raising his glasses, he saw a man in a chauffeur's uniform detach himself from the bonnet of a large, black Mercedes and approach him. *"Pardon, Monsieur,* you are going to the Château Morgue?"

Monsieur Pamplemousse nodded. "That is what I had hoped to do. It is not easy."

The man motioned him toward the car. "I am here to take you. We had word of the *manifestation.* Herr Schmuck sends his compliments."

Monsieur Pamplemousse rapidly revised his view of Narbonne. It was a city he remembered fondly—the birthplace of Charles Trenet, singer of love songs. The way he was feeling, the man's words could have been set to music—another contender for the hit parade. The director must have done his stuff. He pointed toward the spot where Pommes Frites was waiting patiently. "That is very good news indeed. I have my luggage over there."

The chauffeur followed him. "I had not expected *Monsieur* would be accompanied," he said, eyeing Pommes Frites unenthusiastically. "I was not told."

Monsieur Pamplemousse unhitched the lead. He was not disposed to enter into an argument at this stage. "It has all been arranged," he said firmly.

The man gave a grunt as he picked up the valise and led the way toward the car. Monsieur Pamplemousse eyed his unexpected benefactor thoughtfully as he followed on behind. His manner wasn't exactly unfriendly; unforthcoming was perhaps a more accurate description. When he spoke it was with a touch of arrogance, rather as though in the normal course of events he was the one who was used to giving the orders.

A moment later curiosity gave way to something rather stronger. As the man bent down to open the trunk, Monsieur Pamplemousse noticed a distinct bulge high up on the left side of his jacket. It *could* have been a well-filled wallet. On the other hand, instinct told him it was not.

He felt for his own wallet. "Do you happen to have change for a two hundred franc note? Two one hundreds, perhaps?"

"*Non.*" There was no question of looking. He consigned the fact to his memory for possible future use. It had been worth a try.

The Mercedes had the kind of luggage compartment, spacious and spotlessly clean, that made his valise look inadequate and shabby, rather as one felt standing in front of a tailor's mirror being measured for a new suit.

Aware of the odd look the man was giving his white stick, Monsieur Pamplemousse tightened his grip on the handle, adjusted his glasses, and slipped back into his role as he climbed unsteadily into the car. He was pleased to see there was a dividing glass between himself and the driver. With a hundred or more kilometers still to travel, conversation might have flagged a little. As he settled himself down alongside Pommes Frites he felt something hard beneath his right buttock. It was a case containing a pair of sunglasses, Bausch and Lomb, of the type with photochromic variable density lenses that change according to the light. In the circumstances they were like manna from heaven. By the time the chauffeur had climbed into his seat the change had taken place. If he noticed anything different about his passenger he wasn't letting on.

There was a faint whirr and the glass panel slid apart. "All is for the best, *Monsieur?*"

"Oui," said Monsieur Pamplemousse. *"Merci."* He caught the man's eyes watching him in the rear-view mirror. He seemed disappointed by the reply, and faintly uneasy, rather as though he had been expecting something more than the bare acknowledgment he'd received. After an uncomfortably long pause, he pressed a button on the dashboard and the panel slid shut again.

As they moved off Monsieur Pamplemousse relaxed and turned his attention to Pommes Frites, or rather to his rear end. Like most dogs, Pommes Frites was a bit of a snob when it came to cars and he was taking full advantage of his newfound status and the fact that the rear window on his side was half open. Eyes closed in ecstasy, he presented a profile to the world in general and in particular to any local inhabitants who happened to be passing, of one to whom such luxury was an everyday event. For the second time that day Monsieur Pamplemousse felt their usual mode of transport was being held up for comparison and found to be distinctly lacking.

As they gathered speed on the highway outside Narbonne he could stand the draft no longer and much to Pommes Frites's disgust, pressed a button on the central console which controlled the electrically operated window.

Perpignan airport flashed by at nearly two hundred k.p.h. The saying was that birds went to Perpignan to die. Monsieur Pamplemousse couldn't help but reflect that if there was any truth in the saying and they carried on driving at their present speed, many would have their wishes granted sooner rather than later.

At Le Boulou they took the D115 and began climbing steadily. He dozed for a while. When he woke it was already growing dark and they were on a minor road. Ahead of them the Pyrénées looked gray and mysterious, outlined against the lighter sky behind, like a child's painting, simple and stark. Snow on the upper slopes shone luminously in the moonlight.

The car headlights picked out the beginnings of a small village, the houses already tightly shuttered for the night. As they shot through the square he spotted a small bar and beyond the *Mairie* some more lights. A moment later it was gone.

Almost immediately they were out of the village and he was about to close his eyes again when they rounded a sharp bend and drove past a parking area on the valley side of the road, the sole occupant of which was a long, black hearselike vehicle. The driver was standing in front of it relieving himself against a rock. Monsieur Pamplemousse had a momentary glimpse of three others dressed in black inside the car. They waved as the chauffeur gave a blast on his horn. Whether or not they had waved in recognition was hard to say, but he had an odd impression that they were waiting for something or someone. Even funeral attendants had to obey the calls of nature, but it seemed an odd time to be abroad.

Monsieur Pamplemousse turned to see if he could spot the name of the village as they passed the sign, but he missed it in the dark. The Mercedes seemed to be totally unperturbed by the steepness of the climb. His 2CV would have been in bottom gear by now and struggling.

Ten minutes later the Château Morgue came into view, its dark bulk remote and impregnable. Probably built originally to keep others out, it now served to keep people in. Not, thought Monsieur Pamplemousse as they swung in through the gates, that there appeared to be anywhere to go other than the village if any of the guests decided to play truant.

The original stone building had been hideously embellished by a monstrosity in the shape of an enormously tall, circular tower. It betrayed itself as a twentieth-century afterthought, and stood out like a sore thumb. Lights blazed from uncurtained windows at the top, but the rest of the building was in comparative darkness. The inmates of Château Morgue must retire early, probably worn out by their treatment.

Before he had a chance to take it all in and absorb the geography of the surroundings, the driver made a sharp turn and, scarcely slackening speed, they hurtled down a spiral ramp into a vast underground garage, which must have been built at the same time as the tower.

As they pulled up beside some lift doors, Monsieur Pamplemousse glanced at the other cars already parked. Wealth radiated from their bumpers. He counted five Mercedes 500 S.E.C.s, two British registered Daimlers and a Rolls-Royce, an obscenely large American car he didn't immediately recognize, a sprinkling of B.M.W. 735s—two with C.D. plates—three Ferraris with Italian number plates, and a German Porsche. Somewhat incongruously a small Renault van with the words *Château Morgue—Charcuterie* on the side was parked in a corner.

The chauffeur opened the rear door for them to alight, removed the luggage from the trunk, and then spoke rapidly into a small microphone let into the wall. It was impossible to hear what he was saying. Seconds later the lift doors slid open. Barely acknowledging Monsieur Pamplemousse's thanks, the man ushered them through the opening, then reached inside to press the button for the ground floor. He withdrew, allowing the doors to close again. For whatever reason, dislike was now clearly written across his face and he seemed glad to be rid of them.

The inside of the lift was small but luxurious, the carpet unusually thick. On the back wall, near the floor, there was a hinged panel of the kind common to lifts in large apartment blocks—easily removable for the transportation of a coffin. It reminded Monsieur Pamplemousse of their encounter on the road a few minutes earlier. Perhaps one of the patients had died. If the truth were known, death was probably never very far away at a health farm. Many of the clients only went there in the first place because they had caught their first whiff of it on the horizon. Early warning signals from on high.

They stepped out of the lift into a circular foyer which was equally luxurious, like that of a small, but exclusive, hotel: discreet and reeking of understated opulence. The flowers in the vases were out of season. A desk stood in one corner. Its only concession to being functional was a row of buttons set in a freestanding remote control panel, and a red push-button telephone alongside it. The large, leather-covered chair behind the desk was empty. The whole atmosphere was like that of certain establishments he'd come across from time to time in the sixteenth *arrondissement* of Paris. Places where anything was obtainable provided you could pay the price, and nothing was ever questioned.

As they stepped out of the lift a man in a short white coat appeared from behind a screen and came forward to greet them.

"Bonsoir." Tucking a clipboard under one arm he gave a tiny, almost imperceptible bow. "Doctor Furze. Herr Schmuck sends his apologies. He hopes to make your acquaintance later. At present he is unavoidably detained with a patient. In the meantime, I am at your disposal."

While he was talking Doctor Furze glanced down at Pommes Frites and, like the chauffeur before him, seemed surprised by what he saw. Again, Monsieur Pamplemousse got in quickly, forestalling any possible arguments. "This is Pommes Frites," he said simply. "We are never parted."

Although Pommes Frites's inflatable kennel was packed away in the bottom of the valise in case of emergencies, he had no intention of revealing the fact for the time being. If

37

there was any talk of his being accommodated in the stables he would resist the idea most strongly.

After a moment's hesitation, Doctor Furze turned and led the way toward the lift. Swiftly, he pressed a sequence of numbers on a panel. Old habits die hard, and Monsieur Pamplemousse found himself regretting that his dark glasses prevented him from making a mental note of them.

Inside the lift the doctor seemed even more ill at ease, rather as if he had discovered something out of place and didn't know quite what to do about it.

"You are busy?" As Monsieur Pamplemousse posed the question he realized he was lowering his guard again.

Doctor Furze seemed not to notice. He pressed a button marked four. "We are always busy in the V.I.P. area. The regular patients are in the main building. You will not be disturbed. Special arrangements can be made if you require treatment."

It was the kind of remark—a statement of fact, that put a full stop to any further conversation.

The lift opened straight into another circular hallway, almost identical to the one on the ground floor, except for four doors let into the perimeter wall. It struck Monsieur Pamplemousse that the lift doors apart, he hadn't seen any in the reception area. Perhaps there was some kind of medieval secret passage.

Doctor Furze crossed the hall and withdrew from his pocket a chain with a bunch of keys on the end. "I trust you will find everything to your satisfaction." He stood to one side to allow Monsieur Pamplemousse and Pommes Frites to enter.

"No doubt you will wish to unpack before you order dinner. I will arrange for your luggage to be brought up. You will find the menu and the wine list in the bureau. The control panel for the television, video equipment, and the electric shutters is beside the bed."

Monsieur Pamplemousse gazed around. It had to be

38

some kind of joke on the part of the director. In the course of his travels on behalf of *Le Guide* he'd been in some pretty plush places, but this one beat the band. Never before had he encountered such unadulterated luxury. The first room alone would have provided more than enough material for a feature article in one of the glossier Paris magazines: wallpaper from Canovas, crystal from Baccarat, Christofle china and silverware. On the far side of the room, through an archway, he could see a king-size four-poster bed and beyond that a bathroom. Another archway opened onto the dining-area with a table already laid, and to its right sliding full-length windows opened onto a balcony. He crossed to look at the view, but a passing cloud temporarily obscured the moon; by daylight it must be breathtaking. He resolved to have breakfast outside next morning whatever the weather.

Perhaps it was all part of a carefully hatched surprise treat on the part of the management. After his last job of work he was due for a bonus. Vague promises had been made at the time, but somehow they had never materialized. If the thickness of the carpet was reflected in the size of the bill, Madame Grante would be throwing a fit in two weeks' time.

Monsieur Pamplemousse suddenly came back down to earth with a bump as he realized Doctor Furze was talking to him.

"As I was saying, you may prefer to dine alone on your first night." Again there was a slight hesitation. "If not, 'arrangements' can be made. If you would like company . . . a girl, perhaps, or two girls, you will find a list of numbers by the telephone." He glanced toward Pommes Frites. "It is short notice, but it may even be possible to arrange something for your dog. You must let me know his interests."

Monsieur Pamplemousse found himself avoiding Pommes Frites's eye. Pommes Frites had an unwinking stare at times, combined with the ability to make it appear as if he were hanging onto every word, almost as though he could understand what was being said. It was nonsense, of course, but disconcerting nevertheless.

"I think we are both a little tired after our long journey." He felt like adding that he would hardly have known what to do with one girl, let alone two, but resisted the temptation. As for Pommes Frites, heaven forbid that he speak for him or his interests, but he shuddered to think what he might make of any local *chienne.*

"As you wish. If you change your mind, you have only to ring." The bow was accompanied by the suspicion of a heel click. "I will leave you now. No doubt you will wish to take a bath."

Doctor Furze opened the door, brought in the valise, which had been left standing outside, and disappeared.

As he undressed, Monsieur Pamplemousse contemplated his reflection in a mirror that occupied one entire wall of the bathroom, a reflection which was unnervingly multiplied many times by another mirror let into the ceiling. One girl? Two girls? What manner of place had he come to? It certainly bore no relation to any of the reports he'd seen lying on the director's desk. Perhaps they, too, had been a subterfuge? Perhaps even now they were laughing their heads off back at Headquarters. He had a feeling that if he'd asked for three girls it wouldn't have presented a problem.

Three girls! Luxuriating in a leisurely *bain moussant,* he devoted his thoughts to the postcards he would send back to the office; they would be a series of progress reports.

What was it the director had said? "The change will do you good, Pamplemousse."

Pamplemousse basked in a euphoria brought on by his surroundings, a euphoria further enhanced by the warmth of the bath and by the oils that accompanied it, by the Stanley Hall of London soap, not to mention a shave in the softest of water, followed by the refreshing sting of an aftershave lotion which bore the name of Louis Philippe of Monaco. He stretched out a toe in order to ease open the hot water tap a *soupçon,* reaching out at the same time for a Kir Royale, lovingly mixed from ingredients found in a well-stocked refrigerator by the bed. If things carried on the way they had begun, his first postcard would be to the director himself. "Regret, problems greater than expected. May need to stay on for further week."

No, on second thought, why stint himself? Why not play Headquarters at their own game? Why not make it two extra weeks? A month at Château Morgue would tide him over a treat until the spring.

They were sentiments which, although unspoken, clearly won the whole-hearted approval of his thought-reading companion in the next room, reveling in the luxury of his new surroundings while waiting patiently for decisions concerning the evening meal. Decisions which, knowing his master as he did, would be made quickly and expertly when the moment came, and in the fullness of time would bear fruit that would make all the waiting worthwhile.

3

Read and Destroy

Monsieur Pamplemousse was in his element. Gastronomically speaking, he couldn't remember having had such an enjoyable time since the occasion shortly after joining the Force when, as a young police officer, he'd been involved in his first big case outside Paris and had found himself being taken to meet Fernande Point at Vienne. Being shown around the great man's kitchen—in those days the Mecca of *Haute Cuisine* and a training ground for many of the great present-day chefs—had been akin to a small boy of the eighties being invited up to the flight-deck of a Concorde.

Since taking a bath, his pen had been fairly racing over the pages of his *aide mémoire* as he set about making preliminary notes for his report. In his mind's eye as he scanned the menu he was already hard at work planning *déjeuners* and *dîners* for the days to come, adding, subtracting, shuffling around permutations of the many delights it contained, so that he and Pommes Frites would reap full benefit in the time at their disposal, bearing in mind also that, if they were to include visits to the gymnasium during their stay, energy lost through unaccustomed exercise would need to be replaced.

The director must have been joking when he talked of *régimes.* Anything less like a *régime* would be hard to imagine. Faced with making a choice for one meal only he would have been hard put to reach a decision, but given that they were staying at Château Morgue for two weeks, hopefully more, he could afford to go wherever his fancy took him. Such an opportunity rarely came his way.

And if the menu was one of the most exciting he'd come across for a long time, the wine list, too, had been chosen by someone with an eye to the good things in life, and possessed of an unlimited budget as well. It was a positive cornucopia of riches. The Bordeaux section in particular read like the pages of that bible of the wine trade, Cocks et Féret. The Lafites, for example, contained every vintage of note stretching back to the turn of the century. There were so many good things it almost made a choice more difficult, rather like finding oneself in the position of being able to go to the theater after a long absence, and finally not going at all through sheer inability to reach a decision. In the end he opted for a bottle of '78 Château Ferrière—from the Médoc's smallest classified vineyard and a comparative rarity. He had never actually tasted it, but from all he had heard it would be a delightful accompaniment to the *Roquefort,* which, since they were in the area, was a must. It would also go well with the main course, earning bonus points from Madame Grante into the bargain for its very modesty.

Monsieur Pamplemousse made the appropriate note in his book and then read it back out loud for the benefit of Pommes Frites, receiving in return a reaction which could only be termed satisfactory. Pommes Frites had a sizable vocabulary of culinary terms, culled from travels with his master. There were certain key words—like *boeuf,* which invariably caused his tail to wag, and it was only necessary

43

to add the word *bourguignon,* and he would be on his feet in a flash and ready for action. In this instance the phrase *Magret de Canard grillé au feu de bois* had the desired effect, and if anticipatory dribbles weren't exactly running down his chin, it wasn't because the choice failed to receive the full support of his salivary glands, but simply the fact that his mouth was so dry from lack of sustenance they were in need of a certain amount of priming first.

In fact, he couldn't really see what his master was waiting for. If the final decision was to have duck grilled over charcoal for the main course, why not get on with it and leave the choice of the *dessert* until later. Desserts were his least favorite part of a meal anyway, and he was a firm believer in the adage that a steak on the plate was worth two meringues in the oven any day of the week.

It was a thought that gradually communicated itself to Monsieur Pamplemousse. Food took time to prepare and cook. Assuming the whole thing wasn't part of some beautiful daydream from which he would suddenly wake, a mirage that would disappear as soon as he reached out to touch it, they were losing valuable time, which would be better spent over another Kir Royale. Taking the hint from Pommes Frites's restless padding up and down the room, he looked for the appropriate button to press for service.

As he did so he caught sight of his white stick and dark glasses and was reminded once again that he had a role to play. Already he had unforgivably let it slip, first with the chauffeur, and then nearly with Doctor Furze. It wouldn't do to let it happen again.

Having pressed the button he was immediately struck by the fact that service in the Château Morgue appeared to be on a par with its other facilities. He'd barely had time to write a few brief words to Doucette on a postcard he'd found amongst some other stationery—it showed a picture of Château Morgue and he marked with a cross what he judged might be his room as he always did—when Pommes

44

Frites paused in his perambulations and pricked up his ears, staring at the same time in the direction of the hall. A moment later he heard the soft whine of a lift coming to rest outside, then the swish of a door opening. Hastily applying the stamp Monsieur Pamplemousse placed the card between the pages of his notebook, slipped the latter into the secret pocket of his right trouser leg, and then sat back, clasping the stick between his knees, hands on top, preparing himself for a discreet knock from without.

Prepared though he was for some kind of entrance, he hardly expected the onslaught that followed. The door burst open and a positive avalanche of people flowed into his room. First, Doctor Furze, white-faced and agitated, still clutching his clipboard, then two others, a man and a woman whom he barely had time to register before, to his even greater surprise, Ananas swam into view. But it was a very different Ananas to the one he had last seen on Toulouse station. With his jacket torn, tie missing, hair dishevelled, he was clearly in a filthy mood.

Before the others had time to speak, he pushed his way to the front and glared at Monsieur Pamplemousse. *"Enfant de garce! Imposteur! Macquereau! Opportuniste!"*

Clearly he was all set to work his way steadily through the entire dictionary of abuse, but before he could progress beyond the letter "O," help intervened in the shape of Pommes Frites. Normally, despite his size, Pommes Frites was of a gentle disposition. He didn't often growl. Growls he kept in reserve for special occasions. But when he did give voice to them they were of a kind that in his time had caused many an adversary to stop dead in his tracks lest it be followed by even worse manifestations of his displeasure. They began somewhere deep inside his stomach and followed what must have been a tortuous path through his intestines, gathering speed as they passed through various Venturi tubes, growing in volume as they entered and left a variety of echo chambers, before finally emerging between teeth which, when bared as they were now, could well have done service as some kind of industrial shredder.

The effect was both magical and instantaneous. Ananas stopped dead in his tracks and backed away, seeking protection from the others.

Doctor Furze spoke first. "I'm afraid there has been some confusion," he said, consulting his clipboard. "A case of mistaken identity." He glanced from one to the other. "Not unnatural in the circumstances." A snort from the direction of Monsieur Pamplemousse's double made the point that he, for one, did not think it at all natural.

"Pardon." There was a flash of gold from a Patek Philippe watch as the third man held out his hand to Ananas. "We will rectify matters immediately. I will arrange with your manager for your luggage to be sent up while Doctor Furze escorts this—other person to his proper quarters." He turned to Doctor Furze who was hovering nervously on the sidelines, keeping a respectable distance between himself and Pommes Frites. "You have the details?"

For once Doctor Furze had no need to consult his board. The information was obviously indelibly etched on his memory. "Block C, room twenty-two, Herr Schmuck."

"Good. See that the change is carried out at once."

"Certainly, Herr Schmuck."

While the others were talking Monsieur Pamplemousse caught a brief flicker pass between the woman and Herr Schmuck; a warning, perhaps? It was hard to say. Her eyes were as black as pitch, unnervingly so.

Herr Schmuck turned and gazed intently at Monsieur Pamplemousse, as if trying to probe behind his dark glasses. Suddenly, his arm jerked up and he clicked his fingers. Monsieur Pamplemousse, who'd been trying to rehearse focusing his gaze somewhere in the direction of infinity, reacted rather more slowly than he might normally have done. But once again he was saved by Pommes Frites, whose second warning growl came sufficiently quickly for

46

it to divert attention away from his reflexive drawing back. To his relief Herr Schmuck seemed satisfied.

"Come, Ananas," he said, taking the other's arm. "You must allow us to entertain you until your suite has been made ready."

Looking slightly mollified, Ananas gave Monsieur Pamplemousse and Pommes Frites a final glare and then allowed himself to be led away. Madame Schmuck, if it were she, followed on behind without so much as a word or a backward glance. Monsieur Pamplemousse was left with the feeling that, if it came to any kind of argument, she would have the final decision. He was also oddly aware of a faint smell of greasepaint.

"If you wish to leave your bag," said Doctor Furze, "I will have someone attend to it."

"Thank you, no." Monsieur Pamplemousse had no desire to lose sight of his valise, particularly as it contained the case belonging to *Le Guide.* Even though the latter was securely locked, he didn't want to run the risk of anyone tampering with it, and the way matters were going anything was possible.

On the way down in the lift he was tempted to inquire if the menu in C Block was the same as the one he'd just been reading, but he changed his mind. Instead, as they emerged onto another floor, he took a firm grip of Pommes Frites's harness. He needed all his faculties in order to concentrate on his role.

"You will find the accommodation a little less luxurious," said Doctor Furze, as he led the way down a long corridor, bare and featureless, with cream-colored walls and cord-carpeting. "The suite you have just been in is reserved for the personal guests of Herr Schmuck himself, you understand?"

Monsieur Pamplemousse understood. Ananas was doubtless at Château Morgue under a reciprocal arrangement. A free holiday in return for a suitable endorsement.

"Your room." Doctor Furze stopped outside a door. "I trust you will be comfortable."

"Comfortable!" As he entered the room, Monsieur Pamplemousse could hardly believe his eyes. "Comfortable!" He was about to hold forth in no uncertain manner, when he realized he was in no position to. But how could the man stand there and utter such falsehoods without even so much as a change of voice? Spartan wasn't the word. Even Pommes Frites, who was rarely bothered by his surroundings, seemed taken aback. Apart from a single bed and a very small armchair, the only other furnishings were a wooden locker, a chest of drawers, a plain uncovered table, and a wooden bench. Thick pile carpet had been replaced by a piece of coconut matting. Through an open doorway in the far wall he could see a bath and a wash basin, alongside which was a set of scales.

"It feels a little—different," he ventured, as he groped his way round the room under the pretence of getting the feel of it. His heart sank. The iron frame of the bedstead felt cold to the touch. "Am I right in thinking the heating has been turned off?"

"*Oui.*" Doctor Furze made no attempt to enlarge on his reply. Instead, he steered Monsieur Pamplemousse gently but firmly in the direction of the bathroom. "While you are in here perhaps you would be good enough to remove your clothing. I will make a note of your weight. We always like to do that on the first evening, then again in the morning. Patients usually notice the difference straight away."

Monsieur Pamplemousse brightened. Perhaps dinner wouldn't be long in coming after all. He wished now he'd ordered the *cassoulet*. It would have been interesting to see how much weight he put on. "That reminds me," he began, "you might like to help me with the menu. It is a little difficult."

"Of course," Doctor Furze picked up Monsieur Pam-

48

plemousse's trousers and hung them on a nearby hook. "You will find it easy enough to remember. Dinner is at six-thirty sharp each evening. I'm afraid you have missed it tonight, but in the circumstances I will see what can be arranged. Normally, for the first five days it is a glass of *eau.*"

"*Eau?*" repeated Monsieur Pamplemousse. "Did you say *eau?*"

"*Eau.*" Doctor Furze helped him onto the scales. "*Chaude,* of course. It comes from our own special spring, which rises beneath the cellars."

"After five days you will be allowed a little fresh lemon juice as a treat." He took a closer look at a digital display panel on the scales and gave a grunt of disapproval. "We are a little unhappy with our weight, *n'est-ce pas?*"

Monsieur Pamplemousse drew himself up to his full height. "We are very happy with our weight," he said firmly. "It is what we are most happy with. May I have my trousers back, please?" He suddenly felt resentful at having to display his failings in a cold bathroom.

"One other thing," Doctor Furze glanced up from his board. "When you wish to use the bath, please let me know and I will arrange for the issue of a plug. It is not," he allowed himself the ghost of a smile, "that we are short of them. It is a simple but necessary precaution. One cannot be too careful. Once the treatment begins to take effect, many of our patients find it all too easy to get into a bath, but in their weakened state they occasionally have difficulty in getting out again.

"Sign here, please." He pushed a pen into Monsieur Pamplemousse's hand and guided it toward the clipboard. "It is an absolution clause. It is *obligatoire!*"

While he was speaking a beeper sounded. Withdrawing a small receiver from the top pocket of his coat, he listened carefully for a moment, then spoke briefly. "*Oui.* I will come immediately.

"I am afraid I must leave you now. *Bonne nuit. Petit dé-jeuner* is at seven A.M. sharp."

Monsieur Pamplemousse gazed at the door as it closed behind the doctor. On the back there was an inscription in four languages, French, German, English and Spanish: NOTHING IN THE WORLD IS FREE—LEAST OF ALL YOUR HEALTH. Underneath was a list of charges for various extra services, of which there appeared to be a great many.

"Petit déjeuner!" A glass of hot water, no doubt. Followed by another glass for *déjeuner*. He could picture it all. It wouldn't even be drinkable. It would be a dirty, filthy, foul-tasting brown liquid. Straight out of the ground and tasting like it. Its diuretic qualities would be lethal. He'd once sampled some at a spa in the Midi and had sworn there and then never to repeat the experience. Even Pommes Frites, who wasn't above stopping at the nearest puddle when he needed to slake his thirst, had turned up his nose.

Ever alive to his master's moods, Pommes Frites lifted up his head and gave vent to a long drawn out howl. It summed up the situation admirably.

Monsieur Pamplemousse gave him an approving pat, reflecting as he did so that with all the resources of the French language at his disposal he would still have been hard pressed to find words strong enough to describe adequately his feelings; it needed a dog of Pommes Frites's sensitivity to come up with exactly the right sound.

For a moment or two he was tempted to go in search of a telephone and call the director. With luck, he might even be able to persuade Pommes Frites to put on a repeat performance down the mouthpiece.

He thought better of it. He'd had enough of groping his way around in dark glasses for one day. That apart, if he knew the director, he would be neither amused nor sympathetic, particularly if he happened to be in the middle of dinner. Dinner! He gave an involuntary groan. Pommes

Frites let out another howl in sympathy. There was a protesting knock on the wall from the adjoining room.

"Merde!" Monsieur Pamplemousse collapsed into the armchair in a state of gloom, memories of the meal he'd so carefully planned all too clear in his mind. His gastric juices went into overtime at the thought of what might have been. His dislike of Ananas grew stronger by the minute. No doubt he was already making up for lost time.

There was a movement from somewhere nearby as Pommes Frites curled up on the floor in front of him, resting his head lovingly across his master's feet. Thank heaven for Pommes Frites. Where would he be without him? How good it was to have the company of a faithful friend in one's hour of need.

Monsieur Pamplemousse closed his eyes while he luxuriated in the warmth which was slowly enveloping his ankles. It was really a question of who cracked first, himself or Pommes Frites. At least he had the advantage of knowing why they were there. Why and for how long they were meant to stay. Pommes Frites had no idea. He wouldn't take kindly to a glass of water for his *petit déjeuner* every morning. Had they still been at home they would be going for a stroll by now—taking the air near the vineyard by the rue Saint Vincent, walking off the after effects of one of Doucette's *ragoûts.* He could picture it all . . .

He sat up with a start. Thoughts of Paris reminded him that with all the things going on that day he had totally forgotten about the letter the director had given him in his office. He felt inside his jacket. It was still there.

The envelope, which bore on its flap the familiar logo of *Le Guide*—two *escargots* rampant—contained a letter and a second smaller envelope made of curiously flimsy paper. The latter was sealed with red wax, embossed with a symbol which rang a faint bell in Monsieur Pamplemousse's head. A warning bell? It was hard to say. Certainly there was something about it that left him feeling uneasy. Intrigued, he decided to put it to one side for the moment while he read the Director's covering note. It was short and to the point.

"My dear Aristide," it began. That was a bad sign. Either the director wanted to curry favor or he had a guilty conscience.

> I trust you will forgive my not being entirely frank with you in my office, but as you will see, there were very good reasons. Walls, Aristide, have ears, and the enclosed is for your eyes only. Even I, *directeur* of *Le Guide,* am not privileged to be apprised of its contents. Therefore, I can only wish you luck in what I assume is yet another of those clandestine "missions" to which you have become so addicted, and for which you have acquired some notoriety. Take care, Aristide. Above all, take care! For once you are on your own. You can expect no help from Headquarters.

The letter, signed by the director in his usual indecipherable scrawl, ended with a postscript. "Two other things while I write. Please assume that until such time as the order is rescinded, you have *carte blanche* with your P39s. Also, once you have read and digested the contents of the second envelope, please destroy it immediately. Both letter and envelope are made of best quality rice paper. If necessary they can be consumed with no ill effects."

"Boiled, fried, or *nature?*" Monsieur Pamplemousse suddenly felt distinctly hard done by as he glanced at his surroundings. How dare the Director say that he had a predilection for "missions" when as far back as he could remember he had always been a victim of outside circumstances. Not a seeker of "missions," but one who had missions thrust upon him whether he liked it or not. The sheer

52

injustice of the remark rankled. As for apologizing for lack of frankness in his office, that was the understatement of the year. He picked up the second letter and held it to the light. For two pins he wouldn't even bother to read it.

As the last thought entered his mind, a slow smile gradually crept over Monsieur Pamplemousse's face. Tearing a small piece off one corner of the envelope, he applied it to his tongue and then lay back and closed his eyes again. It would have been a gross exaggeration to say that it had a pleasant taste. Comparison with Tante Marie's *gâteau de riz* would have been odious. Indeed, there was hardly any taste at all, more a sensation of blandness. All the same, it would serve them all right if hunger got the better of him and he ate the entire letter then and there, unopened and therefore, *ergo,* unread. There had been nothing in the accompanying note to say he *must* read it.

Dwelling again upon his meeting with the Director, other remarks and phrases came back into his mind: remarks about his weight, slurs cast on his physical features, scarcely veiled criticisms regarding his expense account. And when all those failed, appeals to his better nature and to his loyalty, neither of which had ever been held in question before.

With so much on his mind, sleep did not come easily, but gradually Monsieur Pamplemousse began to nod off, and as he did so he relaxed his grip on the letter, allowing it to flutter gently to the floor. It was an act that did not go unremarked by his companion, more especially because it landed fairly and squarely, if lightly, upon his head.

Nudged into instant wakefulness, Pommes Frites opened one eye and gazed thoughtfully at the offending object. A moment later the sound of steady chewing added itself to Monsieur Pamplemousse's heavy breathing. It was not, in Pommes Frites's humble opinion, one of the best nor the most sustaining meals he had ever eaten, but beggars can't be choosers. What was good enough for his master was good enough for him, and if it didn't exactly fill what was now a gaping void, it did at least bridge a tiny gap or two.

Hunger is not the best of bedfellows, and when Monsieur Pamplemousse woke to the sound of coughing, it was also with a sense of remorse. He realized as he sat up with a start that this sprang from a dream he'd been having—and not simply *having,* but actually *enjoying.* As he patted Pommes Frites on the back to relieve him of whatever was stuck in his throat, he could hardly look him in the eye. To have dreamed of a large suckling pig resplendent on a silver tray, an apple in its mouth, surrounded by a pile of fried potatoes, was one thing. To have transmogrified that pig into his own, dear friend was quite another matter. A shameful episode, one he would do his best to forget. Thank heavens he'd woken when he had.

He glanced at his watch and felt even more guilty. It was nearly midnight. Pommes Frites must be dying for a walk. Apart from the brief spell at Narbonne, he hadn't had an opportunity all day.

A moment later the thought was transformed into action as he led the way along a deserted corridor toward a door at the end marked SORTIE DE SECOURS. Opening it as quietly as he could, he let Pommes Frites through and then left it slightly ajar with the end of a mat so that he could come back in again when he was ready. The air outside struck cold and there was no sense in both of them suffering. He would need all his strength in the next two weeks. What a blessing he hadn't sent off a card to the director. With his present luck the request for an extra two weeks would have been granted.

Leaving Pommes Frites to his own devices he hurried back to his room. Before leaving Ananas's suite he'd had the foresight to pack a few magazines he'd seen lying about. They would help while away the time. Poor old Pommes Frites—he wondered what he was thinking about it all.

Pommes Frites, as it happened, had several very clear thoughts occupying his mind; three, to be precise, and for one not overgiven to exercising his gray matter unnecessarily, three was quite a lot.

The first thought he'd taken care of on a large bush immediately outside the door, and very rewarding it had been too. He felt much better and ready for action. He was very glad his master had made a move, otherwise he might not have been responsible for his actions, for his second thought had to do with bones. Inasmuch as Pommes Frites ever felt guilty, he was feeling it now.

He hadn't been quite so hungry for a long time, and he'd been finding it increasingly difficult to rid himself of a picture that had entered his mind while lying at his master's feet. In his mind's eye he'd suddenly seen them in quite a different light; not as objects on the end of the trouser-covered legs he had known and loved for many a year, but as bones—two lovely, juicy bones. And the longer he'd dwelt on the thought the more juicy and desirable they had become. It had been a narrow squeak. If Monsieur Pamplemousse had stayed asleep much longer he might have woken with an even greater start.

Pommes Frites's third and most constructive thought was that if his master wasn't prepared to do anything about their present situation then he, Pommes Frites, would have to take matters in hand personally. Unlike many of his human counterparts, it was not part of his philosophy to believe that the world owed him anything. The idea wouldn't have entered his head. That being so, when things weren't going right you did something about it. Which, as he set off, nose to the ground on a tour of investigation, was exactly what he intended.

It was some while later, almost an hour to be precise, that Monsieur Pamplemousse, having spent much of the intervening time searching for his letter and finding, to his growing concern, only a small piece of wet and partly chewed red sealing wax, heard a bump in the distance. A bump which was followed almost immediately by the sound of something heavy being dragged along the corridor.

Thinking it might be another patient in difficulty, an elderly lady perhaps, who was suffering from a surfeit of hot water, he put down his magazine with a sense of relief. Any diversion was better than none at all. Without exception the magazines had been porn, certainly not pure, but definitely simple in their single-minded approach to a subject that was capable of almost infinite variations. The only feeling of lust they inspired in him was the wish that some of the many *derrières* displayed could have been real. Had they been real he would have been sorely tempted to take a large bite out of them, so great was his hunger. That would have wiped the smile off some of the owners' faces as they peered around the side, or in some cases from below, tongue protruding from between moistened lips.

By the time he reached his door the thumping was almost outside. As he opened it, Pommes Frites pushed his way past dragging a large parcel tied up with string. His face wore the kind of expression that befitted a bloodhound whose trail had led him to exactly the right spot at precisely the right time.

Having looked up and down the corridor to make sure the coast was clear, Monsieur Pamplemousse closed the door. He had no idea what the parcel contained, but at a guess, since the outside bore the name of a retailer, and below that the magic word *charcuterie,* it might with luck be a delivery of groceries. How and where Pommes Frites had managed to get hold of it was academic. The important fact was that somehow or other he had.

With trembling hands, Monsieur Pamplemousse carried the parcel over to the table and pulled the string away from the outside, up-ending the contents as he did so. To say that he was taken aback by the result was to put it mildly. Even

Pommes Frites looked startled. Putting his paws up on the table he gazed down open-mouthed as a string of sausages spilled out; large ones, small ones, medium sized—as they landed so they seemed to grow in size until it was hard to believe that the parcel he had been carrying could have contained so much.

For a moment or two Monsieur Pamplemousse stood transfixed, a look of wonder on his face. He couldn't remember having seen quite so many sausages since he last attended the annual *Boudin* Festival at Mortagne-au-Perche. There were more than enough to feed a regiment. Then he sprang into action.

Undoing his valise, he removed a smaller case, the one containing the emergency kit issued to all those who worked for *Le Guide*. Designed to cover every eventuality in the minimum of space, it was a miracle of compactness; not a single cubic centimeter was wasted. Spare notebooks, maps, report forms, and writing instruments were contained in the lid. Below that was a felt-lined tray for the Leica R4, two spare lenses—wide and narrow angle, a motor winder, and various filters and other accessories. Below that again, other compartments contained a pair of Leitz Trinovid binoculars, a compass, map magnifier, water purifying tablets (Monsieur Pamplemousse slipped several into his pocket, they might come in useful later), and a book containing emergency telephone numbers. Last but not least, in the very bottom of the case there reposed a funnel, a small butane-operated folding stove, a collapsible pan, and a box of stormproof matches.

In all his years with *Le Guide* he'd never had occasion to use the last three items. Nor, for that matter, had any of his colleagues, as far as he knew, apart from Glandière, who covered the Savoie region and sometimes disappeared for weeks at a time.

Now he blessed the man who had designed it. A man of

foresight, a leader among men. He turned and looked down as something long and sinewy began slapping the side of his leg.

"Pommes Frites!" he exclaimed. "You are *très, très méchant.*" But the tone of his voice gave lie to the words, and Pommes Frites's tail began to wag even faster as he followed his master into the bathroom in search of some water.

Quite frankly, in order to save time, he would have been perfectly happy to dine on a smoked or dried sausage; a *Saucisson de Lyon,* for example, or perhaps one from *Arles,* even a raw sausage or two, but if his master intended cooking them first, then so be it.

The stove alight and the water beginning to show signs of movement, Monsieur Pamplemousse turned to the difficult task of deciding on an order of priorities. With such a wealth of sausages at his disposal, the choice would not be easy. As a member of several distinguished societies—the A.A.A.A.A., the *Association Amicale des Amateurs d'Andouille Authentique, La Confrérie des Chevaliers du Goûte-Andouille,* whose energies were directed toward the perfection of the *andouillette,* not to mention the *Confrérie des Chevaliers du Goûte-Boudin,* who were very protective about that other classic of French *cuisine,* and the *Frères du Boudin Noir et Blanc*—his loyalties were divided.

In the end, much to Pommes Frites's approval, he decided on a representative selection. One by one, *Andouillette, Saucisse de Toulouse, Saucisse d'Alsace-Lorraine, Saucisse de Campagne,* and *Boudins Noirs et Blancs* disappeared into the bubbling water until the pan could hold no more.

Monsieur Pamplemousse thought the *boudins* looked particularly mouth-watering. He'd once taken part in the annual competition at Manziat to see who could eat the most —the winner had eaten over a meter at one sitting. The way he was feeling at that moment, that year's champion would have been an also-ran, a non-starter.

Reaching into the bag again, he took out a fork and

plunged it into the bubbling pan. The *boudin* was beyond his wildest expectations; it would have more than upheld a reputation which stretched back into history as far as Homer. Made to the classic formula of fresh pork fat, chopped onion, salt, freshly ground pepper and spices, pig's blood, and cream, it positively melted in the mouth, like a soft ice cream on a summer's day.

Wiping the juice from his hands lest they soil the pages, he reached for his notebook. The panful in front of him had barely scratched the surface of the vast quantity still left on the table. It would be a useful exercise to start a study of the subject. Already he could see another article in the staff magazine. *Saucisses et Saucissons—A Comparative Study in Depth* by A. Pamplemousse. Perhaps, looking at the pile in front of him, with the words "to be continued" at the end. The editor would be pleased.

At his feet, Pommes Frites gave a sigh of contentment. Oblivious to the subtle difference between an *andouillette* with its quota of chitterlings and tripe, and an *andouille* with its addition of pork meat, he'd had two of each and enjoyed them both. Now he was looking forward to rounding things off with a *boudin* or two followed by a nap. It had been a long and tiring day, a day of ups and downs, and a good nap wouldn't come at all amiss.

It was a thought that appealed to Monsieur Pamplemousse too, and shortly afterward, having taken the precaution of inflating Pommes Frites's kennel and placing it in the bathroom lest he get any ideas about sharing the bed, he started to get undressed. Soon, they were both in the land of dreams.

4

The Camera Never Lies

Monsieur Pamplemousse slept late into the following morning. When he finally woke, it was to the sound of engines revving, the metallic slamming of car doors, dogs barking, and raised voices.

He sat up and looked at his watch. Ten o'clock! *Merde!* Such a thing hadn't happened in years. Breakfast would have been over and done with hours ago. Then he realized where he was. Breakfast was of academic importance.

Getting out of bed, he crossed to the window and drew the curtains. In the driveway near the main entrance a police van was parked alongside the car in which he had arrived. A solitary *gendarme* occupied the passenger seat, otherwise all was quiet. The view was away from the Pyrénées, southward toward the Massif du Canigou and its sacred mountain. Château Morgue was even higher than he'd expected—above the tree line. The surroundings looked as still and unspoiled as they must have been in the days when the Troubadours roamed the area crying *"oc"* instead of *"oui."*

He opened the door to the corridor and peered out.

That, too, was deserted. Outside several of the rooms reposed a tray with a solitary empty glass. The exit door at the far end was ajar, as it must have been all night. He shivered. No wonder it felt cold. Seeing it reminded him that Pommes Frites would probably be wanting to obey the call of nature. Having seen him safely on his way, he turned his attention to the more immediate matter of running a bath. Once again he had cause to bless the man who had designed the survival kit. In a special hole let into the side of the case he found a multipurpose waste plug. Nothing had been forgotten.

As he lay back in the bath he contemplated his changed fortunes. It was certainly a case of one law for the rich and another for the less affluent. Gone were all the expensive unguents and lotions of the previous bathroom. The only aids provided for those who wished to cleanse themselves were a small bar of soap bearing the name of one of the giant combines, and a plastic shower cap. Perhaps not many inmates bothered to ask Doctor Furze for a plug. He could hardly blame them.

The disappearance of the letter was a problem and no mistake. He could hardly blame Pommes Frites, who had doubtless taken his cue from watching his master consume a corner of the envelope. All the same, it wouldn't be very easy to explain. It would be bad enough in writing, but harder still when it came to the interview which would undoubtedly follow. He could picture the looks he would get and how his simple statement—"Pommes Frites ate it" would be repeated in tones of utter disbelief, followed by stony silence. On the other hand, saying he'd lost it wouldn't go down too well either.

For a moment or two he toyed with the idea of phoning the director, but then he dismissed the thought. The director was obviously as much in the dark as he was. He would get no help from that quarter, and it would only bring closer the moment he was trying to put off. Far better to play things by ear for the time being. Let matters take their course.

His musings were broken into at that moment by a double click from the outside door, heralding Pommes Frites's return from his morning stroll. Pommes Frites was good at opening doors. It was a trick he'd learned on a training course when he'd first joined the Paris police. He was less good at closing them again, although in this instance politeness, or discretion, had obviously won the day.

A head appeared around the corner of the bathroom door. Its owner was wearing a distinctly thoughtful expression, but by then Monsieur Pamplemousse was much too busy drying himself to notice.

A leisurely shave and it was time for breakfast. Soon *Saucisses Viennoises,* that heavenly mixture of pork, veal, fillet steak, and coriander, were bubbling away on the stove. He leaned over as one of them rose to the surface, and pricked it with a needle to prevent it bursting.

While he was waiting for them to finish cooking he cut some slices from a *Saucisson de Bourgogne.* The slight tang of the kirsch flavoring would act as an excellent appetizer. Instinctively he made a note about the *saucisson* in his book. It was the correct length—forty-five cm—and had been well dried—in his judgment, six months at the very least. He gave it full marks, as did Pommes Frites from the speed with which it disappeared. The only unsatisfactory aspect was the lack of bread. The smell of freshly baked bread suddenly wafted into his mind. Back home the second baking at the *boulangerie* in the rue Marcadet would be just about ready. Nevertheless, given the circumstances, he couldn't grumble. It had been a more than satisfactory start to the day. Apart from orange juice and coffee, he doubted if even Ananas had fared better.

Washing-up completed, the emergency bag securely locked and packed away, he wrapped the remaining sausages in his overcoat and stowed them away at the back of the cupboard.

Since Château Morgue obviously didn't believe in their patients enjoying the luxury of having locks on their doors —probably in case any of them shut themselves in and lacked the strength to get out again—he hung the OCCUPÉ notice on the outside handle for safety. One couldn't be too careful.

Shortly afterward, holding onto Pommes Frites's harness with his left hand and grasping the white stick with his right, he set off, tapping his way along the corridor away from the SORTIE DE SECOURS toward what an arrow on the wall referred to as the CENTRE D'ÉTABLISSEMENT THERMAL (TOUTES DIRECTIONS). They had dillydallied long enough. It was time to take the bull by the horns and make their entry into the world of *La Cure*.

The signs on the doors of the adjoining building made gloomy reading. Everything from the coccyx to the pharynx seemed to be catered for. There was hardly a part of the body that didn't have its name written up in large capital letters. LES ECZÉMAS embraced LES ACNÉS, and the two jostled for pride of place alongside LES ULCÈRES. Parts of the body he hadn't dreamed existed were displayed in the form of illuminated x-rays, looking more like sliced portions of *andouillette* than anything remotely human. By the time he reached the end of the corridor a strange feeling of itchiness on his skin had been replaced by a dull pain in his stomach. He wasn't sure whether it was a surfeit of sausages or merely psychosomatic, but whichever it was it quickly transmitted itself to Pommes Frites who stopped scratching himself in favor of looking for a possible exit door.

Monsieur Pamplemousse decided that impurities of the skin and intestinal disorders were not high on his list of priorities that day. Far better to get adjusted to his new surroundings with the help of something less exotic.

63

Following a sign marked AUTRES DIRECTIONS, he turned a corner and spied a door marked OBÉSITÉ. His entry triggered off a flurry of squeals and indignant shrieks as a plethora of female bodies scattered in all directions, like over-fat mice at harvest time.

Monsieur Pamplemousse focused his attention on the nearest and undeniably most nubile of the forms. He touched his forelock with the end of his white stick.

"Pardon, Monsieur," he exclaimed. *"Est-ce la bibliothèque?"*

A giggle of relief went around the room. Towels were released and fell to the ground unheeded, their owners breathing sighs of relief as they relaxed again.

It gave Monsieur Pamplemousse a chance to make a closer study of the scene. Like a small boy let loose in an ice cream parlor, he sampled a chocolate-nut sundae here, a banana split there, discarding a half-eaten Knickerbocker Glory to the right of him in favor of a pecan and hot fudge confection to his left, while yet leaving room to maneuver in case he had another change of mind and dipped into a tutti-frutti special. The woman he'd spoken to came toward him.

"I think you have made a mistake."

Essaying a half-hearted attempt at sounding confused, Monsieur Pamplemousse stammered his apologies as she turned him around and gently but firmly pushed him back out through the door. He poked his head back inside for one last, lingering look. From the rear she was even more desirable. "A thousand apologies, *Monsieur,"* he called.

Monsieur Pamplemousse went on his way with a lighter step. Life had suddenly taken on a new dimension. Quick thinking sometimes brought unexpected rewards. Saying he'd been looking for the library had been a mistake, but in the general excitement no one seemed to have noticed. There was no doubt about it, his "affliction" had its compensations.

Farther along the corridor he came across another door

marked GYMNASE. Deciding that violent exercise was not what he was most in need of at that moment, he was about to resume his perambulations when he heard a commotion coming from inside the room. It was followed almost immediately by the sound of an alarm bell ringing somewhere in the distance. Under the pretext of trying to get his bearings, he remained where he was and almost immediately his patience was rewarded. Two men in porter's uniforms came hurrying along the corridor pushing a wheeled stretcher. With scarcely a glance in his direction they opened the door to the gymnasium and disappeared inside, closing it behind them.

Intrigued, he hung around trying to decide whether or not he should follow them, when the matter was decided for him. The door opened and they emerged, moving rather more slowly than they had when they arrived, for the very simple reason that the stretcher now bore the unmistakable shape of a body covered in a white sheet.

As the men carefully maneuvered the trolley through the doorway and into the corridor they were followed by a gaggle of white-faced women clad in leotards. Clearly all were in a state of shock as they squeezed their way past, some averting their gaze, others crossing themselves as they paid their last respects.

In the confusion, Monsieur Pamplemousse groped his way forward and managed to make sufficient contact with the sheet to pull it a little to one side. He found himself looking down at the face of an elderly woman. She looked ominously still, her eyes dark green and lifeless against the white of her skin. There was something vaguely familiar about her. But before he had time to do anything more than record the fact, Herr Schmuck appeared in the doorway.

He seemed slightly thrown off balance by the encounter. Once again Monsieur Pamplemousse was thankful for the variable density dark glasses. The lenses had adjusted to the harsh overhead fluorescent lights of the corridor, affording him a better opportunity to study the professor than he'd had the night before. Herr Schmuck looked a good deal older than he'd thought. His skin had the kind of waxy sheen, like tightly stretched parchment, common to the very old. He was also considerably less in command of the situation than he had been on the occasion of their last meeting. Once again, there was a faint smell of grease paint.

Taking advantage of the momentary pause, Monsieur Pamplemousse tapped the floor impatiently with his stick. "Will someone please tell me what is going on? I do not understand. Has there been an accident?"

As he spoke he reached over toward the motionless figure on the stretcher. Almost as though he was anticipating the move, Herr Schmuck beat him to it. In a single movement he closed the woman's eyelids and pulled the sheet back over her face, but not before Pommes Frites managed to give it a quick lick. He seemed somewhat surprised by the result, rather as though it had left a nasty taste.

Herr Schmuck signaled the two men to carry on. "My apologies for this unfortunate encounter. There is no cause for alarm. It happens from time to time. Normally we try to carry out these unpleasant tasks as discreetly as possible, but alas . . ." He gave a shrug as he hurried after the others.

Monsieur Pamplemousse watched the progress of the stretcher party along the corridor, one man pushing, Herr Schmuck and the other man following on behind. Speed seemed to be the order of the day. So much so, as they went to turn a corner at the end they narrowly missed colliding with Doctor Furze who was coming the other way. His inevitable clipboard went flying and while he bent down to pick it up Herr Schmuck paused in order to exchange a few words.

Monsieur Pamplemousse was left in no doubt as to the subject of the conversation. Several times they turned and looked in his direction and at one point Herr Schmuck said something that clearly caused a certain amount of ribald amusement amongst the others.

Doctor Furze nodded, beckoned to one of the two attendants to follow him, and came hurrying down toward the gymnasium. Monsieur Pamplemousse turned to go on his way, but he had left it too late. Before he had time to take more than a few steps the other two came up on either side of him and he felt his arms being grasped gently but firmly. He tried to free himself, but the grip tightened.

"Ah, Monsieur Pamplemousse. I am pleased to see we have begun our treatment. That is good." Doctor Furze's voice had unpleasant overtones.

"Merely a preliminary survey. A voyage of exploration. Pommes Frites and I are getting our bearings." Monsieur Pamplemousse tried to conceal a growing uneasiness by making light of the matter. "Or rather, Pommes Frites is getting *his* bearings. As ever, I merely follow on behind."

"Then it is as well we came along." Doctor Furze made a pretense of consulting his clipboard. "You are down for a workout in the gymnasium this morning. A little toning-up of the muscles is indicated before you start your course. We have machinery for such things." He made it sound like "We have ways of making you talk."

"It is, I am afraid, the moment when you and Pommes Frites will have to part company for a while. As you know, *chiens* are *interdits* at Château Morgue. An exception was made in your case, but there are certain areas where we cannot bend the rules. Others would complain."

While he was talking Doctor Furze pushed open the door to the gymnasium and before he had time to remonstrate, Monsieur Pamplemousse found himself being propelled through the gap. There was a click as the door closed behind them, followed by a dull thud as Pommes Frites applied his full weight to the other side.

"Good. You appear to have the room to yourself." Ignoring the interruption, Doctor Furze punctuated his remark with a metallic click as he operated a catch on the door. "We must make sure you are not disturbed."

Torn between wanting to protest and the need to preserve his masquerade, Monsieur Pamplemousse inwardly registered, but passed no comment on, the paraphernalia of keep-fit gadgetry surrounding him: rowing machines, stationary cycles, parallel bars, apparatus he'd only ever seen adorning the pages of glossy magazines.

Deciding that discretion was, for the time being at least, the better part of valor, he allowed himself to be helped onto a machine whose purpose he would have been hard put to define had he been asked. It looked more like the cockpit of a space module than anything remotely connected with keeping fit.

A moment later, as he lay back in a semiprone position and felt leather straps being tightened around his ankles and wrists, he wished he hadn't given in so easily. But he had left it too late. As Doctor Furze reached up and pressed a button on a panel mounted to one side of the machine, he felt his legs begin to move in a kind of pumping action, slowly at first, then gradually gathering speed. At the same time his outstretched arms were carried upward over his head, then inexorably back again. The doctor flicked another switch and there was a sudden surge of power.

Closing his eyes, Monsieur Pamplemousse was dimly aware of voices and vague movements in front of him. Then they disappeared and he heard a door close.

Fighting back the feeling of utter helplessness which came over him as he realized he was on his own, he concentrated all his efforts on trying to ride with the machine rather than resist it, knowing that if he once allowed himself to falter, panic would set in. He was determined not to give Doctor Furze the satisfaction of seeing him in a state of collapse when he returned. *If* he returned. The memory of the woman on the stretcher came flooding back and he

wondered if she, too, had found herself in the "hot seat."
It had certainly felt warm when he'd first climbed onto it.

How long his ordeal might have lasted, Monsieur Pamplemousse had no means of knowing. All he was aware of were clouds of a reddish color filling his brain; redness, followed by purple, then total blackness enveloped him as he passed out. It was followed by a feeling of floating on air and an unaccountable warmth, a perfumed warmth which came from somewhere overhead.

He opened his eyes and saw first Pommes Frites, or rather Pommes Frites's tongue as it reached out to lick him, and beyond that an impression of peaches, a peachlike skin covered in soft down.

"Are you all right?" The peach swam into focus and formed itself into a face. "What an awful thing to have happened. Thank goodness your dog kicked up such a fuss. I found him trying to scratch the door down. I can't think how it could have been left locked. Luckily I had my pass key with me."

While she was talking the owner of the face set about undoing the straps and Monsieur Pamplemousse realized for the first time that the machine was no longer working.

As the last of the straps fell away he tried to dismount, then he fell back again as his legs started to buckle beneath him.

"You'd better come back to my room." The voice took charge and a hand reached out to take hold of his. "What I still can't credit is that anyone could be so careless. It would be bad enough at the best of times, but to let it happen to someone in your condition!"

"My condition?" Monsieur Pamplemousse suddenly remembered he had a part to play. He groped around with his free hand in search of his stick. Pommes Frites, ever alert to his master's needs, picked it up in his mouth and handed it to him.

"My room" turned out to be farther along the corridor

and far enough away from the gymnasium for Monsieur Pamplemousse to breathe more freely. As far as he was concerned, the farther away the better.

He stole a quick glance at the inscription on the door as it was held open for him. It bore the name COSGROVE. MRS. ANNE COSGROVE. The label said, PÉDICURE ET MASSAGE. Below the name there was a list of appointments for the day. He considered the matter for all of a hundredth of a second. A few minutes earlier he would not have remotely considered having his toenails attended to, let alone subjecting himself to a massage, and yet . . . instinct told him it was an offer he shouldn't refuse.

Mrs. Cosgrove held the door open and very gently placed a hand on his left elbow. She was wearing a white suit, which must have been stock issue as he had seen other staff wearing it, but somehow she managed to make it seem as though it had been specially tailored. Perhaps it was because she had made certain modifications. The zipper, which ran the length of the jacket front, from the high-collared neck down to the bottom hem, had been replaced at some time by one in bold, black plastic, with a large ring attached to the fastener. The sleeves were short, the trousers beneath closely fitting and held firmly in place by a figure that was both full and inviting.

"I'm afraid I do not have an appointment. It is perhaps a case of—how do you English say?—pot luck." As he allowed himself to be led into the room, Monsieur Pamplemousse drew on the small stock of phrases remembered from his stay in Torquay. In England at that time there had been a lot of pot luck.

"Oh dear." Mrs. Cosgrove smiled ruefully. "Is my accent *that* bad?"

"Not at all." He was about to say he had seen her name on the door, but he stopped short in the nick of time. Instead, as she took hold of his hand to guide him into a waiting chair, he essayed a compliment. "You have the skin of an Englishwoman—it is very smooth and flawless."

It was true. As she leaned over and he felt the warmth of her body close to his he was reminded once again of peaches. Peaches and cream on a hot summer's day by the Marne, or perhaps even more appositely, on the banks of the river Thames, Henley, perhaps, where the English had their boat races.

"When you have the misfortune to inhabit the world in which I live," he said simply, "you acquire an extra sensitivity." Out of the corner of his eye he caught sight of Pommes Frites watching him intently, hanging on his every word. He turned the chair slightly on its swivel. Pommes Frites could be very off-putting at times.

"Gosh, yes. I suppose so." Mrs. Cosgrove sat down on a stool in front of him and began removing his shoes and socks. "Is it true what they say about blind men then?"

Monsieur Pamplemousse felt himself heading toward deep water. "People say many things about many people," he said noncommittally. "Some are true, some are not."

Mrs. Cosgrove crossed one leg over the other as she reached over toward a tray of instruments. Her free leg began to swing to and fro like the pendulum of a clock. According to Didier in Planning it was a sure sign of some deep frustration, and he should know. He'd been married three times.

"I mean about their being good lovers." Mrs. Cosgrove hastily uncrossed her legs and lifted his right foot onto her lap. "I suppose I shouldn't really have said that."

"It is a question you would have to ask of another woman," said Monsieur Pamplemousse. He gritted his teeth as Mrs. Cosgrove set to work, first on the instep, then gradually moving up toward the ankle. It felt as though his foot was on fire.

"George has got very good eyesight."

"George?"

"My husband."

"He is here?"

Mrs. Cosgrove gave a hollow laugh. "I should be so lucky. No, he's at home, in England. He doesn't hold with this sort of place. Too much like hard work. He's probably out shooting or fishing."

Monsieur Pamplemousse digested this latest piece of information, trying to form an equation between a man who was rich enough to spend his time out shooting and fishing on the one hand and on the other a woman massaging his ankles in a remote corner of France. Perhaps Didier was right in his theory and it accounted for the frustration.

"Life goes on." Mrs. Cosgrove was one step ahead of him. "They say a change is as good as a rest. I took a course years ago. Not," she continued with feeling, "that it's doing me much good. I seem to spend most of my time either fending off geriatric foot fetishists or digging toenails out of the curtains."

"Every occupation has its hazards," said Monsieur Pamplemousse. "And few people are without their problems."

Mrs. Cosgrove sighed. "You can say that again. This place is full of them. It's funny really."

"Funny?"

"Well, it's the first time I've worked anywhere like this, but it isn't at all what I expected. It's on two levels, if you know what I mean. Half the patients are barely tolerated—almost as if they are a necessary evil. They come and they go and then they are forgotten, whereas the privileged few get treated like lords. You hardly ever see them. When they arrive they have their own separate garage and they disappear into the Tower Block. But you try going up there if you haven't been invited."

Monsieur Pamplemousse pricked up his ears. "You have been?"

72

"I tried once. You'd have thought I was trying to rob Fort Knox. All hell broke loose."

"And how about the other patients? Are there many who don't last the course?" Monsieur Pamplemousse related his experience outside the gymnasium that morning.

Mrs. Cosgrove looked as if she had heard it all before. "That's the second this week. It's a regular occurrence. They've a set routine. The flag over the entrance gate gets lowered to half mast. Old Schmuck puts on his black arm band. Then the hearse arrives and carts the body away and everything returns to normal as if nothing had happened.

"Mind you, they probably die happy, which is more than a lot of old dears can say. He can turn on the charm when he likes. He calls them his 'investments' and he certainly makes sure they get their dividends."

"Is it usually women?"

Mrs. Cosgrove paused for a moment. "You know, it's funny you should say that. I've never really thought about it before. I don't remember it being a man. Not while I've been here anyway. Mind you, it's a matter of statistics. A lot of rich old widows come here simply because they're lonely. Rich old widowers don't have the same problems."

Monsieur Pamplemousse closed his eyes. His mind was starting to fill with facts. Facts that needed sorting and relating one to the other. Not for the first time he wished that Pommes Frites had the power of speech. There had been something odd about their encounter with the stretcher party in the corridor, something he couldn't for the moment quite put his finger on. Pommes Frites had sensed it too, of that he was sure. It came to him suddenly. Herr Schmuck had already been wearing an arm band. He must have been very quick off the mark.

Mrs. Cosgrove glanced up at him. "I must say your glasses are a bit disconcerting." She reached for his other foot. "I can't tell at all what you're thinking."

"I was thinking it would be nice to see you again." It wasn't strictly true. He was also feeling that an ally on the staff would be a great asset. "Perhaps when you have finished for the day?"

Mrs. Cosgrove lowered her head. Her hair, he noticed, was fair down to the roots—a natural blonde. The nape of her neck looked eminently kissable.

"Staff are not encouraged to fraternize with the patients."

"And if they receive encouragement from them?"

"Then it is expressly forbidden."

"That is a great pity."

"What block are you in?"

"C."

"Mine is the adjoining block. Room thirteen. I usually have a workout around four o'clock. We could have tea together afterward."

Monsieur Pamplemousse rose. Thirteen was his lucky number. He would leave the rest of his toes until another day. It would be good to have something in reserve. And when Mrs. Cosgrove was through with them, had he not read somewhere that the human foot contains something like twenty-six separate bones, not to mention all the attendant joints, ligaments, muscles, and supporting tissues? More than enough to cover the rest of his stay at Château Morgue.

"Shall we say four-thirty then?"

"Make it a quarter to five. I'll leave early and pop down to the village for some cakes. You must be starving." Mrs. Cosgrove held the door open for them and once again, as she touched his elbow he felt her warmth. *'A bientôt.'*

"A toute à l'heure."

Monsieur Pamplemousse bowed and hobbled on his way, conscious of her eyes following him as he tapped his way back down the corridor. Aware, too, of a certain reserve in Pommes Frites's manner, an aloofness that hadn't been there previously, as he led the way, looking neither to the right nor to the left.

Safely around the corner, Monsieur Pamplemousse bent down and gave him a pat. The response was lukewarm to say the least. He sighed. It was to be hoped there would be no unpleasantness. If they were to share a room for the next two weeks that was the last thing he wanted. Besides, he was going to need all the help he could get.

The rest of the journey back to the room was carried out in silence. Pommes Frites clearly wanted to draw a veil over the whole proceedings, whilst Monsieur Pamplemousse, struggling to keep up with him, allowed his mind to dwell on other problems.

Apart from some minor youthful sorties in Torquay, it was his first real encounter with an Englishwoman, and he had to admit that many of his preconceptions and prejudices had received a severe dent. In no sense of the word, *par exemple,* could Mrs. Cosgrove have been called "cold"— something he had always been brought up to believe about her compatriots. Nor was she in the slightest bit "angular." Again, very much the reverse. A trifle "horsy" perhaps; she had a generous mouth and slightly protruding teeth. He could picture her on a winter's morning astride some galloping steed, clutching the reins with one hand, a whip in the other— its flanks tightly gripped between her thighs, its nostrils steaming. Perhaps hers would be too.

As they reached their room Pommes Frites brought his daydreams to a sudden halt. On an instant he froze into a position which Monsieur Pamplemousse had good cause to remember from many occasions in the past. It was as if a spring had been tightly coiled. A spring that powered twelve point five kilograms of muscle, flesh, and bone, cocked and ready to be released at the slightest signal from his master.

Someone was inside their room.

Monsieur Pamplemousse let go of the harness, carefully removed his dark glasses and placed them in his top pocket, then stood back and prepared for action. He felt a tingle of excitement as his grip tightened on the door handle. It was quite like old times. Turning the latch so slowly it was almost impossible to detect any kind of movement, he waited until it was down as far as it would go and then pushed against the door with all his might.

As it shot open and they entered the room it would have been hard to say who was the most surprised, the sole occupant or them.

"Do you always come through doors like that?" Ananas exclaimed petulantly, leaping to his feet. To say that he looked as if he'd been nearly frightened out of his wits was to put it mildly.

"Do you make a habit of entering other people's rooms without first receiving an invitation?" retorted Monsieur Pamplemousse. He took a quick glance around. Everything seemed to be in place.

"Touché." Ananas pulled himself together. "Normally, no." He crossed and pushed the door shut. "The fact is, I didn't want to be seen hanging around outside and I didn't know where you were. Also," he added cryptically, "I feel we should not be seen together."

Without waiting for a reply he sat down and began mopping his brow with a silk handkerchief. He looked strangely ill at ease, not a bit like the blustering Ananas of the previous evening.

"To tell you the truth, I'm in a spot of bother and I wondered if you could help."

"Me?" Not by the wildest stretch of his imagination was he able to picture how he could possibly help Ananas, a man who seemed to have everything, including friends in the highest places in the land. Nor, for that matter, did he, for the moment at least, see any good reason why he should.

"I know you, Pamplemousse. You are a man of the world. I know your *past* reputation." The emphasis on the penultimate word did not escape Monsieur Pamplemousse.

"Why you are here, masquerading as a blind man, is not my concern. No doubt you have your reasons. And no doubt your little pretense is something you wish to keep to yourself."

Monsieur Pamplemousse felt a growing impatience. He had not liked Ananas from the very beginning; now his dislike increased with every passing moment. "Would you mind coming to the point?"

Ananas took the hint. He reached into an inside pocket and withdrew some photographs, which he tossed onto the table. "The point is . . . these. They were placed in my room this morning."

Monsieur Pamplemousse picked up the top one and glanced at it. His first thought was that someone, for whatever reason, had been to a junk yard and taken a picture of a pile of old statues.

"You are holding it upside down," said Ananas impatiently.

Monsieur Pamplemousse rotated the photograph and gradually, as he examined it more closely, a kind of pattern emerged from the montage of arms and legs and thighs and breasts. It was obviously some kind of orgy, but an orgy of such enormous complexity it was hard to tell who was doing what and to whom.

"Mon Dieu! Sapristi!" An involuntary whistle escaped his lips. Only one part of the whole was clearly identifiable and that was the head in the middle. It was Ananas coming up for air. He looked at the other man with renewed respect. "When was this taken?"

"Last night. I was feeling a little . . . restless. Traveling always does that to me." It was said so matter-of-factly it almost took Monsieur Pamplemousse's breath away. He thought of his own travels and they paled into insignificance.

"The trouble is," Ananas had the grace to look slightly shifty, "they're mostly under age."

"Under age?" Monsieur Pamplemousse took another look at the picture. *"C'est impossible!"*

"Si." Ananas peered over his shoulder. He pointed to one of the legs. "That one is fourteen. Her sister there is only thirteen."

Monsieur Pamplemousse gave another whistle. "And that one? She looks thirty-five if she is a day."

Ananas took a closer look. "Ah, yes, that is the mother. They are all a bit, you know. . . ." He tapped his head as if in doing so it absolved him of all blame. "It comes through living in the mountains. The long winter months when they are snowed in. There is a lot of inbreeding.

"Anyway," he dismissed the subject. "The important thing is, someone is obviously trying to blackmail me. It is a warning. Next time there will be a note. It is not the first occasion and I cannot afford a second. It would mean the end of my career. Absolute discretion is essential—the local police must not be brought in. I have given the matter a great deal of thought and you are the ideal person for the job."

"Non!" cried Monsieur Pamplemousse vehemently. *"Non! Non! Non!"* With each exclamation he brought his fist down on the table with a thud. "Give me one good reason why I should do such a thing."

"Because," Ananas took the photograph and held it up with the air of one about to play his trump card, "people in dark glasses should not throw stones.

"It is my recollection that when you left the Sûreté it was under a cloud owing to some indiscretion at the Follies. How many girls was it? Thirty-two?"

Monsieur Pamplemousse snorted. "A trumped-up charge. I resigned as a matter of principle."

"Nevertheless, mud sticks. There are many who still believe what they read in the *journaux.* Those same people will be quick to recognize the face in this photograph. They will think not of Ananas, but of Pamplemousse. I must admit that the supposed likeness is something I, personally, cannot see, although it has caused me some irritation in the past. Some comparisons are more odious than others."

Monsieur Pamplemousse gazed in disgust at Ananas as his voice droned on. He had no intention whatsoever of submitting to what was, in effect, a secondary form of blackmail, nor did he feel any great desire to render help to Ananas. On the other hand, to have his true identity revealed, not that of Pamplemousse, late of the Sûreté, but Pamplemousse, representative of *Le Guide,* would be a disaster. It would negate all his past work; it would be a betrayal of all that he now held dear. He decided to play for time.

"I will consider what steps should be taken," he said stiffly.

"Bon. I knew you would understand." Ananas reached out as if to shake him by the hand, but Monsieur Pamplemousse pretended to misunderstand. There were lengths to which he was not prepared to go. Instead, he picked up the rest of the photographs, detached one for safe keeping, and handed them over. "No doubt you will wish to keep these as souvenirs."

Ananas paused at the door and gave a conspiratorial wink. "We are in this together, *n'est-ce pas?"*

Monsieur Pamplemousse barely suppressed a shudder. The thought of being in anything together with Ananas was not a pretty one.

"You will hear from me in due course," he said gruffly.

As the door closed he sat down on his bed and considered the next move. It was two o'clock. Two and a half hours before he took tea with Mrs. Cosgrove. He studied the photograph again. How much nicer the single English peach than a whole bunch of wild Pyrenean berries.

He lay back and closed his eyes, wondering if it would be Indian tea or China. Monsieur Cosgrove was probably a retired tea planter. There were a lot of them in England.

He probably had it shipped over regularly. Either that, or Earl Grey. Earl Grey from Fortnum & Mason. He'd seen it on sale in Fauchon. Yes, that would be it: Earl Grey tea, *pâtisseries,* and Madame Cosgrove. It was something to look forward to. Something to dream about in the intervening period. Ananas and his problems could wait. One thing was certain—they would not go away.

5

Tea for Two

After a brief lunch of *Saucisses de Périgord,* followed by some *Saucisson à l'Anis*—a little known variety he hadn't come across before, and which occasioned yet another note in his book—Monsieur Pamplemousse set off with Pommes Frites to reconnoiter the grounds of Château Morgue.

From the outside and in daylight, it looked even more forbidding, but as a retreat or fortress it was ideally situated. Built on a craggy tor, with the land falling away steeply on three of its sides, the only practicable approach was from the south, up the narrow winding road along which they had traveled the night before.

The Hautes Pyrénées were much nearer than he'd realized. He resolved to look at a large-scale map of the area when they got back to the room so that he could pinpoint their position exactly.

He glanced up at the tower, wondering at the same time if he was being watched. There was no particular reason why anyone should bother. There were others around, taking the air as he was. It was simply that his white stick and dark glasses made him feel conspicuous. He was also aware that his coat smelled strongly of sausages. He hoped there were no guard dogs around.

The bottom half of the tower was almost windowless. Only the rooms on the upper floors saw the light of day, and they must be all of sixty meters from the ground. Anything might be going on up there. Anything—or nothing. He wished more than ever now that he'd taken note of the sequence of numbers Doctor Furze had used to operate the lift, so that he could find out at first hand.

A path ran around the outside and he was just about to set off along it when he heard the sound of an approaching car, followed a few moments later by the crunch of tires on gravel. Walking back the way they had come he was just in time to see a hearse disappearing down the ramp into the underground garage. There were four men inside it. He was too far away to be certain, but he could have sworn one of them—the driver—was the man he'd seen relieving himself against a rock the evening he arrived.

He waited and after a while his patience was rewarded. There was a whine and the hearse reappeared, the occupants sitting respectfully to attention. As it went past he instinctively reached for his hat, then stopped himself in time, but not before he'd confirmed his suspicions. It was the same men, probably in the same car, for that too had borne a Marseilles registration number.

Reflecting on how easy it was to take sight for granted, and how hard life must be for those who have lost it, having to rely on others for even the simplest scraps of information, Monsieur Pamplemousse was about to call it a day and go back inside, when he noticed that while his back was turned someone had already been at work over the entrance. The flag, which had been at half mast when he began his walk, was now fluttering at the masthead again. The whole episode had only lasted a bare two or three minutes. Herr Schmuck wasn't joking when he said they tried to carry out such operations with discretion. Or, as Mrs. Cosgrove might have put it, they had got things down to a fine art at Château Morgue.

He felt Pommes Frites give a tug at the harness. The message was clear and to the point. He glanced at his watch. It showed 16:40. Time for tea. Tea and Mrs. Cosgrove.

Whatever else might transpire, whatever undercurrents might be read into his invitation, the thought uppermost in Monsieur Pamplemousse's mind as they made their way to the adjoining block, was that cakes of any description would make a welcome change from sausages.

He yielded to no one in his love and admiration for the sausage in all its many forms and variations, but deep down he had to admit that as a day-to-day diet, *sans* any kind of vegetable, or even a slice or two of bread, to help them on their way, they had their limitations. More than ever, he was also looking forward to some liquid refreshment.

They arrived at Mrs. Cosgrove's at almost the same moment as she did. Fresh from her workout, she was dressed in a white track suit, and if at first she seemed a trifle taken aback to see Pommes Frites, she quickly recovered.

"I suppose you have to take him with you *wherever* you go," she said brightly, as she opened the door for them. "Even indoors. I mean, I suppose he's always with you, sort of . . . watching over you, seeing what goes on?"

"Always," said Monsieur Pamplemousse firmly. "We are inseparable. Without Pommes Frites, pouf!"

"Yes, of course." Mrs. Cosgrove eyed Monsieur Pamplemousse's companion somewhat nervously. He was wearing his inscrutable expression, his eyes following her unwinkingly around the room as she hurried to and fro, drawing the curtains, placing a chair ready for his master and spreading a cloth over a small table by its side.

"I'll get everything ready and then if you don't mind I'll just take a quick shower and slip into something a bit more comfortable. I feel as if I've been put through a wringer."

As she disappeared momentarily behind a cupboard door Monsieur Pamplemousse seized the opportunity to carry out a hasty inspection of his surroundings. The room was very little different in size to his own, but there the similarity ended. Apart from an air of semi-permanence, which perhaps wasn't surprising, it reflected another, more private and slightly unexpected side to Mrs. Cosgrove's character. Despite her slightly horsy, outdoor appearance, she was clearly very much into frills. Frilly doilies decorated the dressing table, matched by other frills along the edges of shelves and the bedside cupboard. The bed itself was even more extravagantly embroidered, a plumped-up *soufflé* of blue silk, edged with white lace. It looked soft and inviting, as far removed from his own orthopedic mattress and plain thin quilt as it was possible to imagine. Altogether a very feminine room.

The dressing table was festooned with knickknacks and ornaments, from the center of which the slightly incongruous, grayish figure of a man in a trenchcoat against a leafy background stared at him from the surround of a black picture frame. He had his coat collar turned up, rather as if it had been raining when the photograph was taken, and he was peering in through a window.

Monsieur Pamplemousse's guess as to the man's identity was confirmed a moment later when Mrs. Cosgrove removed the picture in passing and deposited it face downward in a drawer. Irrationally, he felt a sense of relief as she pushed the drawer firmly shut.

"I do hope there's enough to go around," she said pointedly, as she placed a plate piled high with cakes on the table beside him. "I hadn't expected three to tea and there isn't time to go down to the village again. Besides," she lowered her voice conspiratorially, "I'll be for it if they find out. Patients aren't allowed in the staff quarters. They're out of bounds." She made it sound like a schoolgirl prank.

The temptation to say that as far as he was concerned the cakes looked exactly what the doctor might have ordered was hard to resist. *Babas, éclairs,* almond creams lay alongside *mille-feuilles* oozing with layers of *crème-chantilly;* it was a veritable symphony of the *pâtissier's* art. He could hardly wait.

Pommes Frites had no such inhibitions. He smacked his lips noisily as he peered at the table.

Once again Mrs. Cosgrove eyed him regretfully. "Do you think he wants to go walkies?"

"Walkies? *Qu'est-ce que c'est* 'walkies'?" Monsieur Pamplemousse tried to get his tongue around the unfamiliar word.

"Une promenade. By himself. I could be your 'eyes' while he's gone. That is, if you'll let me."

Monsieur Pamplemousse tried to picture persuading Pommes Frites of the need to go "walkies" while there was a plate of cakes waiting to be eaten. He shook his head.

"It is very kind of you, but no."

"Oh, well." The rattle of teacups as Mrs. Cosgrove rummaged in the cupboard was tinged with disappointment; it was also mixed with the clink of bottles.

Monsieur Pamplemousse shifted slightly so that he could get a better view. As he did so he caught his breath. He could hardly believe his eyes, but there in front of him, as large as life and twice as beautiful, he could see several bottles that were unmistakably from Champagne. Behind them stood a row of high-shouldered bottles, which could only contain Bordeaux, and to one side—he shifted the other way—there was a bottle of Cognac. Not ordinary, run-of-the-mill Cognac, but a single vineyard Marcel Ragnaud. He knew it well, although it was not often he had the pleasure of drinking it.

"Do my old ears deceive me," he asked casually, "or can I hear the sound of glass?"

"You can." Mrs. Cosgrove opened the door wider still

and removed one of the bottles. She placed it gently onto a shelf alongside two glasses. "I'll put one out. Perhaps we can have it later. It's a Gruaud Larose '66 and I hate drinking alone."

"A *Gruaud Larose soixante-six!*" Monsieur Pamplemousse repeated the words reverently, savoring each syllable—almost as if he was sipping the very wine itself. It evoked memories, one of the great wines of that year.

"George always says, if you're going to be a wino at least do it in style. He never was much of a one for plonk."

Monsieur Pamplemousse's opinion of the British and of Monsieur Cosgrove in particular went up by leaps and bounds.

"Madame Cosgrove . . ." he began.

"Do call me Anne."

"Anne." He felt slightly embarrassed. It was a long time since he'd asked a woman to call him by his Christian name. In the Auvergne, where he was born, there were people he'd grown up with who still called him by his surname. To such people informality came very slowly. "You may call me Aristide."

"Aristide!" There was a chuckle from the direction of the bathroom. "I thought only people in school textbooks were called Aristide. There used to be one in mine—he had lots of uncles and aunts and he was always wanting the window open. I grew up thinking French people had a thing about fresh air." Her voice became slightly muffled. There was a hiss of water from the shower.

"You were saying?" She came back into the room, lifted the frilly cover of a wickerwork basket and dropped the top half of her gym suit through the opening. There was a wriggle and the bottom half joined it. Monsieur Pamplemousse drew in his breath sharply. Mrs. Cosgrove was quite, quite naked. *En tenue d'Adam,* as the expression went.

"I was saying . . ." He groped in the dark recesses of his mind for some clue as to what he might possibly have been saying and came up with nothing. *Sacré bleu!* He must take a grip of himself. "I am sorry. It could not have been important."

Legs wide apart, Mrs. Cosgrove stood in front of a full-length mirror for a moment or two pinning up her hair and then, catching sight of Pommes Frites watching her in the glass, she turned and hurried into the bathroom. The sound of the water changed.

"Do forgive me," she called. "I shan't be a moment."

"Please, take as long as you like." Monsieur Pamplemousse gave his glasses a quick wipe and then settled back in his chair, contemplating the stream of water as it cascaded down, over and around Mrs. Cosgrove, finding valleys here, seeking out fresh pastures there, changing course rapidly as she bent down to pick up the soap, then surging forward anew, carrying a mountain of foam before it as she lathered herself all over with a series of sensual, sucking noises.

Any pangs of conscience he might have had about his deception were quickly quashed. Without taking his eyes off the scene for a second, he reached out for a cake.

"That's good. I'm glad you've made a start." Mrs. Cosgrove stood facing him in the doorway, rubbing her back briskly to and fro with a large towel.

"It's a bit of a bore doing gym, but George always says I must look after my best features."

Monsieur Pamplemousse wondered which features George put top of his list. It would make interesting reading. From where he was sitting there were a number of highly desirable contenders. Did he place great store on Mrs. Cosgrove's firm but generous *balcon,* each *poitrine* topped by a nipple still erect from its final dousing in cold water? Or was he, perhaps, an *homme* addicted to the delights of the *derrière*? As Mrs. Cosgrove turned and bent down to dry her toes he had cause to find his own list of priorities wavering. It was undoubtedly a *derrière* of considerable distinction. An *arrière-train* to be reckoned with, and one, moreover, which was also extremely close. He could have reached out and touched it. By his side he sensed Pommes Frites, nose twitching, entertaining what were probably not dissimilar thoughts. Anticipating his possible intentions, he laid a restraining hand on his head.

Mon Dieu! He felt for his handkerchief. Mrs. Cosgrove would never know how close she had come to being defiled. For no particular reason he found himself wondering how Alphonse would have coped with the situation. By now he would probably have dissolved into a pool of melted wax.

"I say, are you all right?" He suddenly realized she was talking to him again. "You've gone quite pale. And your glasses are all steamed up. Not that that matters, of course!" She covered her embarrassment with a nervous giggle as she realized what she had said. "Forgive me. I keep forgetting."

Monsieur Pamplemousse pulled himself together. "It is nothing. Merely the steam from the shower." He wiped the lenses clean and then sat back, pretending as best he could to fasten his gaze on the bathroom wall behind Mrs. Cosgrove, but somehow the tiles refused to come into focus.

"You are being very quiet." She opened the wardrobe door and began searching inside. "Is anything wrong?"

"The art of speech was given to us to conceal our true feelings," said Monsieur Pamplemousse primly. It wasn't entirely apposite. In fact the more he thought about it the more he wondered why he'd said it, but it bridged a gap.

"I say, that's very clever." Mrs. Cosgrove ran something black and lacy through her fingers, then discarded it.

Monsieur Pamplemousse wondered if he should confess that Voltaire probably thought so too when he first coined the remark, then thought better of it. He had other matters on his mind; matters not entirely unconnected with his hostess's present behavior.

Mrs. Cosgrove's liking for frills obviously extended beyond the decor of her room. One by one, undergarments made of silk, chiffon and nylon, in all possible shades of color from lavender blue to the deepest of black, beribboned and lace-edged, came under her scrutiny and were rejected for one reason or another.

Monsieur Pamplemousse sat bemused. He wondered what the director would have thought had he been there to see him. It was the kind of fashion show one read about in glossy magazines, but never in his wildest dreams had he pictured being present—in the very front row as it were—at such a display; a display that said as much about the workings of Mrs. Cosgrove's mind as it did about the whims and mores of the world of fashion.

Having narrowed the choice down to two alternatives, and having weighed the relative merits of loose-layered black against whiteness and tightness and decided in favor of the latter, she sat on a stool, garter-belt in place, and slowly and lingeringly drew on a pair of white stockings.

As she stepped into the briefest and flimsiest pair of matching *culottes,* Monsieur Pamplemousse reached automatically for yet another cake and found to his horror that there were only two left. He also noted a change of mind on Mrs. Cosgrove's part. The wearing of *culottes* was patently not the order of the day; an unnecessary embellishment. She had stepped out of them again.

"Poor Aristide." Mrs. Cosgrove's voice cut across his thoughts. "I've been neglecting you."

The blue of her dress matched the rest of the furnishings. A transformation had taken place. She could have been dressed for afternoon tea on a lawn in England. The knowledge he possessed produced a strange feeling of intimacy. Paradoxically, to take advantage of it, even to tell someone else, would seem like an act of betrayal.

"Ça ne fait rien." He brushed aside her apologies as he adjusted to the change. "I have been very happy with my

thoughts. And with your delicious *pâtisseries* too, I must confess."

"That's good." She reached into a handbag and took out a lipstick. "You must have been starving. What with being on the *régime* and all that excitement this morning."

"Excitement?" The morning seemed an age away.

"That trouble in the lecture hall. I see she's been whipped away already. You didn't happen to notice her legs, did you?"

Monsieur Pamplemousse shook his head, wondering what snippet of information he was about to receive next.

"I bet they were huge compared with the rest of her body. They've all had huge calves—like a ballet dancer's. One of the attendants told me.

"If you ask me, old Schmuck's after their money. Either that, or he's turning them into meat pies or sausages or something."

Monsieur Pamplemousse suddenly choked on the remains of his cake. "What makes you say that?"

"Oh, I was only joking. That would be a bit too much like Sweeney Todd. It's only that they seem to run a *charcuterie* business on the side. Funny combination really." Satisfied with the state of her face, Mrs. Cosgrove turned away from the dressing-table mirror. "How about a cup of tea? Or a Beaumes de Venise?"

It didn't take him long to decide. There was really no choice. Mrs. Cosgrove's revelations had triggered off an urgent need for alcohol. He was also aware of a change in the atmosphere. If he wasn't careful they would be into the area of making polite conversation.

Mrs. Cosgrove obviously felt it too as she began searching amongst a collection of cassettes in a case beside her bed. A moment later, as she went to the cupboard, the strains of "Some Enchanted Evening" filled the room. Pommes Frites gave a deep sigh.

"I'm sorry it isn't chilled. If I'd thought, I could have

stood it outside on the windowsill. The thing is, in England we drink it at the end of a meal. Whereas in France . . ."

"In France it is drunk more as an *apéritif*, something to stimulate the appetite." Monsieur Pamplemousse tried to leap the first hurdle. "Unlike most other wines it is aged in concrete, not wood. It helps to retain the special flavor."

The glass was large, the helping generous. He raised it to his nose; the perfume had opulence. He glanced at the label. It was a Domaine de Durban from Jacques Leydier.

As he felt the smooth lusciousness of the golden-amber liquid at the back of his throat he began to feel better again. He drank it rather too quickly, aware that Mrs. Cosgrove was only sipping hers as she gazed at him thoughtfully over the top of her glass. He was also aware once again of the swinging leg syndrome. He wondered what she was thinking. How hard it was to read a woman's mind. Perhaps she was waiting for him to make the first move? He reached out a hand.

Mrs. Cosgrove pushed the plate of cakes toward him. "Do finish them up."

"*Non, merci.* It is for you."

Pommes Frites cast a reproachful look in his direction as Mrs. Cosgrove took him at his word. Monsieur Pamplemousse pretended not to notice. In many ways he envied Pommes Frites his simple approach to life. He would have summed up the situation in a trice. Not for him the soft music, nor the Beaumes de Venise; garter belts he would have regarded as an unnecessary hazard—something he might catch his claws in. If he saw what he fancied, that was it. The worst that could happen was a bucket of cold water —like that time in the rue Ordener.

Mrs. Cosgrove ran her tongue round the edge of the last remaining *mille-feuille.* She made it look like the dress rehearsal for some more lascivious activity to come. He felt his pulse quicken as she sank her teeth slowly into the pastry.

"Scrumptious!"

Monsieur Pamplemousse waved his hand noncommittally through the air. He was not familiar with the word. "Pastry is like mayonnaise. It is largely a matter of temperature. It needs a marble slab chilled with ice, the best butter, but most of all it is a question of *tour de main,* the 'feeling in the hands.' It is something you either have or you do not have. The best chefs always do it in the early morning."

"George used to like doing it in the early morning," said Mrs. Cosgrove sadly.

"He is a chef?" Monsieur Pamplemousse tried to picture Mrs. Cosgrove's husband in the kitchen. It wasn't easy. He seemed inseparable from his trenchcoat.

Once again, for some reason, the spell seemed to be broken. Perhaps it was his own fault this time for getting involved in culinary matters. As if to underline the fact there was a click from the direction of the bedside cabinet and the tape came to an end. It must have been set at an appropriate spot, for it had only lasted the length of the song. In the silence that followed he heard a car door banging somewhere outside. Mrs. Cosgrove crossed to the window and parted the curtains slightly.

"It's the police. They are back. Apparently there was a break-in during the night. Someone got into the kitchens and stole a lot of food. I heard on the grapevine that the police think it was an inside job and they're planning to make a room to room search."

She let the curtain fall into place and then turned back into the room. "I say, are you *really* all right? You're looking quite pale."

"It is nothing." Monsieur Pamplemousse struggled to his feet and reached for Pommes Frites's harness. "I think perhaps I will go and lie down for a while."

"You are welcome to stay here." Mrs. Cosgrove tried hard to keep the disappointment from her voice.

"Merci." Monsieur Pamplemousse reached out for her

hand and gave it a quick squeeze. "It is better that I return to my own room. Perhaps . . . perhaps you would like to visit me later when it is quiet?" He lowered his voice. "I will let you sample my *andouillette. En suite,* we can drink the wine you have so kindly put out. If you open it now it will give it time to breathe."

"Would *you* like that?" As she spoke he felt her hand tighten on his.

"It would give me very great pleasure," he said simply.

She led him to the door and planted the lightest of kisses on his right cheek. It was like the touch of a *papillon*'s wings.

"Au revoir, Aristide. Until . . . later."

"Au revoir . . . Anne." He found it hard to make the changeover to her Christian name.

Pommes Frites gave an impatient tug and a moment later they were on their way. Once around the corner leading to the adjoining block Monsieur Pamplemousse quickened his pace. There was not a moment to be lost.

Sensing that all was not well, Pommes Frites entered into the spirit of things and by the time they reached their own corridor there was no holding him. As it was, they reached the safety of their room only just in time. As Monsieur Pamplemousse closed the door behind them he heard voices coming from the next room, voices coupled with the opening and closing of cupboard doors.

Merde! There wasn't a second to lose. By the sound of it they were making a thorough job of things.

Jamming his stick under the door handle, he rushed to his own cupboard, removed the parcel of sausages from his coat and tipped them out on to the table. As he looked around the room his heart sank. He would have done better to have made a clean breast of things with Mrs. Cosgrove and left them with her for safe keeping. It was too late now.

Grabbing a knife, he sliced a *Saucisson de Bourgogne* in half and placed the two pieces in a pair of socks. They would do service as a draught excluder along the bottom of the door.

He tried slipping some *Saucisses de Bordeaux* into the hem of the curtains, but in his haste they stuck halfway. Ever anxious to help, Pommes Frites pulled them out again. Then, flushed with success, he made a dive for one of the socks.

In desperation, as he heard *au revoirs* and apologies being voiced in the corridor outside, Monsieur Pamplemousse picked up the remaining sausages and hurled them through the opening of Pommes Frites's kennel. Hardly able to believe his good fortune, Pommes Frites bounded in after them.

"Non!" Monsieur Pamplemousse rapped out the single word of command in a voice which left no room for argument. *"Asseyez-vous. Gardez les saucissons!"*

He was tempted to add *"Gardez les andouillettes avec un soin particulier,"* but he decided against it. At such moments beggars could hardly be choosers and Pommes Frites looked confused enough already. As his jaw dropped open with surprise at his master's sudden change of mood, a half-eaten *boudin* fell out. Honesty, precision, and simplicity of phrasing were necessary in issuing orders of the day, and Monsieur Pamplemousse knew that given those three factors his wishes would be respected without question.

Covering the front of Pommes Frites's kennel with a large towel, he closed the bathroom door, hurriedly pushed the socks back into position under the main door, then sank back into his chair. As he did so there was a peremptory knock from outside.

Adjusting his glasses, Monsieur Pamplemousse focused his gaze on a point somewhere beyond the Hautes Pyrénées and prepared himself for the worst.

"Entrez, s'il vous plaît." Much to his surprise, his voice sounded almost normal.

6

The Leading Role

There was a scuffling noise outside the door, followed by a muttered imprecation from the person on the other side, then another knock, this time even louder and more peremptory than the first.

"Ouvrez la porte, s'il vous plaît." It was a command rather than a request.

Monsieur Pamplemousse jumped to his feet. *Sapristi!* He had forgotten the stick. The door had been pushed with such force it had momentarily risen sufficiently to trap one of the socks containing the *Saucisson de Bourgogne* when it came down again. Already meat was showing through a weak patch in the toe, threatening to burst through the seams at any moment. He should have used a *Mortadella,* it would have been harder.

"Un moment!" The stick bent as he used it as a lever in order to force the door up. There was an ominous crack. A second later the socks were free. Two more and the window was open. He hurled the offending items out into the night. Almost immediately there was a loud bark followed by the sound of snarling as they landed near some unseen target.

The police must have brought their dogs with them. Mercifully they had not yet penetrated the building.

Closing the window, he took advantage of the momentary lull to put his own weight against the door, removed his stick, and then stood back waiting for the storm to break.

The door opened and four people entered the room. Doctor Furze, a police inspector and two *gendarmes*. Monsieur Pamplemousse looked at them in surprise. From the rumpus outside he'd expected a whole army.

Doctor Furze eyed him suspiciously. "Do you make a habit of barricading your door in this manner?" he demanded. "The locking of doors is strictly forbidden at Château Morgue."

Monsieur Pamplemousse decided that attack was the best form of defense. "When I feel threatened, yes. I have heard there have been, shall we say, 'goings-on' during the night. I was merely taking precautions to safeguard my person. Someone in my position cannot be too careful.

"Anyway, who are you and what do you want? I recognize your voice from last night, but who are the others?"

"Furze here." Raising his voice in the way that people sometimes do when talking to the blind, as if they must suffer from deafness as well, the doctor made it sound like a disease. "The others are Inspector Chambard and his two assistants."

Monsieur Pamplemousse nodded. From his looks he judged Inspector Chambard to be from the Midi or the Rhône Valley; he had a short, stocky figure and a face weatherbeaten by years of exposure to the Mistral. Not someone to fool around with—his eyes were too shrewd.

"To what do I owe the pleasure?"

Doctor Furze gripped his clipboard a trifle nervously. "As you so rightly say, there was a little unpleasantness during the night."

"An important package has been stolen," Inspector Chambard cut in. "It is believed that the person responsible

96

may well be a resident of the Château. In the circumstances we feel that for the sake of peace all around there will be no objection if we make a search of the entire building."

"Who knows where or when the thief may strike again?" agreed Doctor Furze. "It is a necessary precaution."

"And if I object?"

"Then we cannot, for the moment, insist." Inspector Chambard's remark was accompanied by a shrug that said it all. Refuse and our suspicions will be aroused. And if our suspicions are aroused then we will be back with the necessary authority within the hour. Take it or leave it. There was a time when he would have reacted in exactly the same way.

"Please." His gesture embraced the whole room. Somewhere outside a dog began to choke noisily. In a flash the window was open again and Inspector Chambard disappeared through it. He returned after a moment, climbing over the sill with an agility surprising for one of his bulk. He held up the half-eaten remains of something green and woolen.

"It appears to be a sock."

"Tccchk!" Doctor Furze looked at it impatiently. "Is that one of yours, *Monsieur?* If so, I have to tell you that the hanging of laundry outside the window is—"

"I know. It is strictly forbidden. Many things seem to be strictly forbidden at Château Morgue."

Ignoring the interruption, Doctor Furze looked around the room. "You have a dog."

"Pommes Frites. He is asleep. Or rather, he is trying to sleep." Monsieur Pamplemousse wished he'd thought to put the "Do Not Disturb" notice on the bathroom door. "I take it that is not against the rules?"

"There is also," continued Doctor Furze, "a list on your door of various activities for the day. You are required to report to the doctor to whom you have been assigned for an analysis of the treatment you require. That was not done. May I ask why?"

"You may," thundered Monsieur Pamplemousse. "You may indeed. I did not carry out the instructions for the very simple reason that I am unable to see them; a fact which seems to have totally escaped both you and your staff. I find your attitude totally intolerable. No one, I repeat, no one has been to see me since the evening I arrived. For all you know I might have starved to death."

He groped for the back of the chair. Already he was beginning to feel a little better, more in command of the situation.

Doctor Furze was the first to speak following his outburst.

"There is a cake crumb stuck to your moustache," he said coldly. "Also, there is a lump of something white adhering to your left ear. I trust it is shaving cream and not *crème pâtissière*. In which case, the patch of red on your right cheek will be blood where you cut yourself shaving rather than what it looks like—a lump of *confiture*."

Instinctively Monsieur Pamplemousse reached up to his face, but before he had time to reply he felt himself being propelled toward the bathroom as Doctor Furze pressed home his temporary advantage.

"We do not appear to have had our daily weight check."

"I am *not* getting undressed again," said Monsieur Pamplemousse. "Is there no privacy in this establishment? It is bad enough not being able to lock one's door without having to expose oneself to all and sundry."

"There is no need. All that is necessary is to remove your shoes. I will make the appropriate allowance." He paused and gave a sniff. "For one who has been without food for over twenty-four hours, your breath is remarkably sweet. It is one of the first things one notices about people who are taking the *régime*—the breath."

He helped Monsieur Pamplemousse onto the scales. "Ah, it is as I suspected." His voice grew even harder and colder as he glanced at the dial and then compared the figure with that on a sheet of paper attached to his clip-board. "At the very minimum your weight has increased by over two kilos since yesterday evening."

Leaving Monsieur Pamplemousse to his fate, he went back into the other room where Inspector Chambard and the two *gendarmes* were engaged in an inch by inch search of the furniture.

"You need look no further, Inspector. I suggest you arrest this man immediately."

"With respect, *Monsieur,* you must allow me to be the best judge of that." Inspector Chambard sounded piqued. "We are not looking for someone who has overindulged in *pâtisseries.* If that were the case then in an establishment such as this we would have cause to make many arrests were it a criminal matter. Lack of food makes people desperate. I have heard tales of excursions into the village after dark. If old Pertus who runs the *boulangerie* relied on sales to the local inhabitants for his living he would not be in a position to buy himself a new Citroën every year. No, *Monsieur,* we are looking for someone who stole a large quantity of *charcuterie,* not just sufficient to put on two kilos of weight overnight, but twenty kilos. That is a lot of *charcuterie.'*

Twenty kilos! Monsieur Pamplemousse barely suppressed a whistle as he came out of the bathroom to join the others. No wonder the sausages had looked like a small mountain when he had first tipped them out.

His heart sank as there was a muffled exclamation from somewhere behind him. Pommes Frites's hideaway must have been discovered.

Pushing him to one side, the second *gendarme* went in search of his colleague. He heard their lowered voices coming from the bathroom.

"Regardez!"

"Merde!"

The appositeness of the remark triggered off a series of giggles. He could picture the nudges that went with it.

"C'est formidable!"

"Oui. Très, très formidable!" There was a stream of admiring whistles and "poufs."

"*Qu'est-ce que c'est?*" Unable to stand the suspense a moment longer, Inspector Chambard flung open the door of the bathroom.

"*Sacré bleu! Nom d'un nom!*" His endorsement of their findings was short, sharp, and positive. It was also accompanied by a series of warning growls. Pommes Frites enjoyed a game as much as the next dog, but he was beginning to get a bit restive with the present one.

Monsieur Pamplemousse turned. All three policemen were on their hands and knees in front of the kennel, eyeing the contents with disbelief and its occupant with a certain amount of reserve. One of the *gendarmes,* clearly under a misapprehension as to the nature of his find, held a handkerchief to his nose as he poked at a *boudin* lying on the floor near the entrance with his truncheon. He jumped back as a paw shot out. "*Merde!*"

"What did I tell you?" Doctor Furze bustled into the bathroom, anxious to declare the matter closed. For some reason best known to himself, he seemed to view the finding of the sausages as a mixed blessing, one which, while confirming his previous accusation, held other connotations of a less desirable nature.

Inspector Chambard rose from his knees and came out of the bathroom. Ignoring the doctor, he addressed himself to Monsieur Pamplemousse.

"Will you call off your dog, *Monsieur?*"

"May I ask why? He is doing no harm; merely protecting his temporary home."

"I wish to search it. I may need the contents as evidence. It will be sent for analysis."

"Not without a warrant," said Monsieur Pamplemousse firmly.

Inspector Chambard gave him a long, hard stare, then

shrugged. "In that case . . ." he turned back to the bathroom. "Paradou, since you appear to be an expert on matters to do with *le petit coin,* I suggest you put that knowledge to some purpose. Get to work."

"But, Chief . . ."

"Wrap a towel around your arm. You know the drill."

Paradou looked around for his colleague, but he had already beaten a hasty retreat and was busy looking through the pile of magazines on the table. If he was hoping for sympathy, he was disappointed.

"Chief, come and have a look at this." As Inspector Chambard half closed the bathroom door, the other *gendarme* held up a photograph. Monsieur Pamplemousse stifled a curse. It was a diversion, but not a welcome one. He should have locked it away in his case.

"Hey, Paradou, come here." The *gendarme* was having difficulty in hiding his excitement.

Paradou, his arm partly swathed in a towel, came out of the bathroom with alacrity. He stared at the picture. *"Tante Hyacinthe!"*

Slowly rotating the picture as he held it up to the light, he reeled off more names. "That one is Clothilde and there is Desirée—at least, I think it is Desirée, and that must be little Josephine and . . ." He peered at the head in the center, then at Monsieur Pamplemousse, comparing the two to make sure he'd seen aright.

"Don't tell me you've been with that lot?"

"Who? Where? What are we talking about?" Monsieur Pamplemousse was becoming increasingly irritated by the way things were going. The sooner his visitors left the happier he would be.

But there was no stopping Paradou. "When I was in the army we used to have lectures about steering clear of the local girls. Why? Because they were always poxed up to the eyebrows. Well, in the last war Tante Hyacinthe's mother was a 'local girl,' and in the war before that so was her grandmother. And if there's ever another war, that's where Tante Hyacinthe will be—up front with the troops. She, and all her family."

Monsieur Pamplemousse began to feel profoundly relieved he hadn't taken advantage of Doctor Furze's offer the night before. He wondered if he should pass on the news to Ananas or keep it in reserve.

Doctor Furze himself had been keeping very quiet during the whole of the conversation. He was deep in thought.

"May I ask how this photograph came to be in your possession, Monsieur Pamplemousse?"

"Photograph? There is a photograph?" Aware of a sudden change in the atmosphere, Monsieur Pamplemousse played for time. At the mention of his name the two *gendarmes* exchanged glances, then stiffened as they caught the eye of their superior. He studiously avoided looking at Paradou. "Perhaps it was among the magazines. I heard you rustling them. Really, it is very hard to answer such questions when I cannot even see what you are discussing."

Inspector Chambard came to his rescue. "Paradou, you get back in that bathroom."

"Perhaps, Monsieur Pamplemousse," he continued, "you would like to accompany me to the *Gendarmerie?*" Both his name and the invitation were underlined by a wink. A brief, but very definite wink.

"Am I to understand that you are placing me under arrest?"

"No, but there are things you may wish to discuss."

"In that case, the answer is no."

Inspector Chambard looked disappointed. "If you change your mind . . . if you see the *folie* of your ways, you have only to telephone."

It was an allusion to his past. His fame must have traveled farther than he'd ever realized. No doubt the photograph had clinched matters in Chambard's mind. It would be in character.

"*Merci.* Perhaps later." He had no wish to get involved with the local police for the time being, but there was no sense in putting their backs up.

A thought struck him. "In the meantime, perhaps you could do me a favor?" He felt in his pocket and took out the postcard to Doucette. "It is to my wife. If you would be kind enough to post it for me."

"Of course." The wink as Chambard pocketed the card was even more meaningful. Monsieur Pamplemousse was about to reciprocate when he realized the other couldn't see it, so he removed his glasses and under the pretense of rubbing his eyes used his hand as a shield.

Doctor Furze hovered at the door. "I find all this most unsatisfactory, Inspector. I shall report back to Herr Schmuck and no doubt you will hear further."

Inspector Chambard looked unmoved by the implied threat. He picked up the photograph. "If you don't mind, I will keep this for the time being."

The bathroom door opened and Paradou emerged carrying a plastic bag. Pommes Frites must have relented. "I'll tell you something funny, Chief—"

"Later." Inspector Chambard waved his subordinates on their way. He suddenly seemed anxious to leave. Looking aggrieved, Paradou followed his colleague out of the room.

Chambard looked at his watch. "*Au revoir,* Monsieur Pamplemousse."

"*Au revoir,* Inspector." A moment later they were gone. He heard their voices disappearing down the corridor. Doctor Furze was still holding forth. He looked at his own watch. It said 5:35. There would be time to kill before Mrs. Cosgrove put in an appearance. Time to marshal his thoughts.

Pommes Frites had clearly been trying to marshal his thoughts during the time he'd spent in his kennel. Without a great deal of success, if the furrows on his brow as he came out of the bathroom were anything to go by. The game he had played with the policeman had been enjoyable up to a point, like playing cat and mouse. Several times when he'd laid his paw gently on the man's hand it had produced a satisfactory muffled scream; but it was definitely a spectator sport. It was nothing without an audience and he was glad he'd managed to conceal the bulk of the sausages at the back of his kennel. Now he was ready for action and, patently, action was something that for the time being had a very low priority on his master's agenda. Monsieur Pamplemousse, his brow equally furrowed, was sitting at the table, a pile of forms set neatly in front of him, sucking the end of his Cross pen, torn between two items of work on his immediate agenda.

On the one hand there was his duty to *Le Guide.* So far, apart from one or two desultory scrawlings on his pad, he hadn't made a single note. On the other hand lay the secondary, or for all he knew perhaps even the primary, reason for his being at Château Morgue, and short of paying a visit to the local vet and ordering him to carry out an immediate search for the letter, those reasons would remain entombed in Pommes Frites's stomach—if they hadn't already passed through. He was in a quandary and no mistake.

Not, he reflected, as he gazed at the pile of papers in front of him, that there was anything blank about *Le Guide*'s report forms. Quite the reverse.

They were based on the simple premise that all things are capable of being analyzed provided they are broken down into their basic component parts, like the myriad tiny dots making up the picture on the television screen, each equating its particular shade of color with an equivalent voltage.

Although there was a large section at the end for a written report, the main bulk of the form was taken up by over five hundred basic questions to which the answer was a simple *"oui"* or *"non,"* thus ensuring that despite differences of temperament and taste, all inspectors spoke the same language. Tastes might vary, but standards never. It also provided an insurance against any kind of bribery or corruption, for in the end its findings were unassailable and unarguable, covering everything from parking facilities to the design of the cutlery; from the quality of the ingredients to the size of the portions and the way in which they were served.

Was the dish of classic origins? If so, had it been prepared in the right manner? Was the accompanying sauce too hot? Too cold? Too salty? Was it served separately? Was the waiter able to describe the dish? If not, did he find out the answer quickly and accurately?

There was an equally large section devoted to the serving of wine. Did the waiter simply sniff the cork and pour it straight away, or did he allow you to taste it first? If it was a Beaujolais was it served slightly chilled? If it was an old wine did he offer to decant it? If so, did he do it at the table? Did he use a candle? Did he take it away to do it? If so, did he bring the empty bottle back to show you? Did he bring the cork too? When he offered you some to taste was he really seeking your opinion or merely going through the motions?

The list seemed endless. In his wisdom, Monsieur Hippolyte Duval had provided for almost every eventuality. The one situation he hadn't foreseen was that of being incarcerated in an establishment where the sole form of nourishment appeared to be a glass of dirty water, and not even that much if the guest happened to arrive late.

After staring at it for something like a quarter of an hour, Monsieur Pamplemousse laid it down again. If *Le Guide* was to enter the world of *Etablissements Thermaux* they would need a totally new form and a very truncated one at that.

One of his options disposed of, at least for the time being, Monsieur Pamplemousse turned his attention to the second item on the agenda. Taking a leaf out of *Le Guide*'s book, or rather, borrowing from its report forms, he began analyzing his findings to date, reducing everything to its simplest terms.

Was there something odd about Château Morgue? Most definitely *"oui."*

Was there a Château Morgue that showed one face to the outside world and another that kept itself very much to itself? From his experience the first evening, *"oui."*

Were the "extra facilities" he'd been offered available to all and sundry? If the answer to the previous question was in the affirmative, then it had to be *"non."*

Was the mortality rate at Château Morgue higher than at other, similar establishments? For the moment at least, he had no means of checking.

Was there any significance to be attached to the sex of those who had passed away? Instinct told him there was; logic failed to come up with an immediate reason.

Was there any significance in the size of their calves? An impossible question.

He tried another tack.

Had he been sent there for some deeper purpose than merely losing weight? Had someone heard of his impending visit and decided to take advantage of it? Without knowing the contents of the letter he couldn't be absolutely sure, but deep down he knew the answer.

Once again, he felt tempted to telephone the director and make a clean breast of things. Once again, he decided against the idea. It was a matter of pride. The director would not be sympathetic. He would assume his "I find this difficult to grasp, Pamplemousse," voice:

"Would you mind repeating that more slowly? You say Pommes Frites actually *ate* the letter? While you were asleep? A letter of the utmost importance! A letter from the highest authority!"

Then there would be the sarcastic tone: "You say all those who died recently were women? And they had unusually large *mollets?* Could it be, Pamplemousse, that you are suffering aberrations brought on by lack of food? I have heard this sometimes happens."

This would be followed by incredulity: "What is this I hear? You have *not* been on a *régime*? You have been living on *saucisses* . . . and *saucissons!*" There would be silences. Silences intermingled with splutterings. Perhaps even the sound of banging on the director's long-suffering desk. He could picture it all too clearly.

He stared at his list. In all conscience, it wasn't much to go on, but at least it was a beginning.

Were the staff in general involved? He pondered the question. Starting from the top: Herr Schmuck—certainly, and therefore presumably, the aloof and detached Madame Schmuck. He wondered why she had so little to say for herself. And yet she had the air of being a power behind the throne. Doctor Furze? In all probability—a tentative *"oui."* There had been something odd about the chauffeur, but as for the rest of the staff he had met so far, *"non."* He would have staked his reputation, for example, on Mrs. Cosgrove not being involved.

He found himself staring into space. Rubbing his chin thoughtfully and realizing he needed a shave, he looked at his watch. *Sacré bleu!* He would need to get a move on if he were to make himself look reasonably respectable in time for their *tête-à-tête*. Pommes Frites, too. If Pommes Frites was to be in a fit state to receive Mrs. Cosgrove he would need a good brush and some Vaseline rubbed on his nose; it was beginning to look dry after being cooped up indoors for so long. Mrs. Cosgrove—he still found it hard to think of her by her *prénom.*

His thoughts coincided with a knock on the door. Mrs. Cosgrove was early.

Kissing him lightly on the cheek as she brushed past, she

gave a quick glance around the room; first at Pommes Frites, watching her with a red and jaundiced eye from a position he'd firmly taken up in the center of the rug; then at the furniture, much of which was still as it had been left after the search. Finally, she looked down at Monsieur Pamplemousse's feet.

"I hope I am not too early."

"Not at all." Wishing he'd remembered to put his shoes back on, he went to kiss her hand, then realized she was holding something behind her back.

"I've brought the wine." As she placed an uncorked bottle and two glasses on the table, he took the opportunity of studying her more closely, on home ground as it were. She had obviously spent the time since they'd last met in a more productive manner than either he or Pommes Frites. Her blue dress had been exchanged for a more casual one in cream. Like her uniform jacket, it had a zipper running down the front. He caught a different perfume too. It had a discreet understatement, which left him wanting more. Her hair hung carelessly over her shoulders in a way that could only have been achieved through long and careful brushing.

Her hand trembled slightly as she began to pour the wine. He noticed, too, that she filled her own glass first and took a quick drink before attending to his. He wondered idly if she was still *sans culottes.*

"Merci." He took it gratefully, conscious of a lingering touch from her fingers as they met his. Rotating the glass quickly and expertly, he swirled the liquid around until it touched the rim, then held it to his nose. The bouquet as it rose to greet him was full and fruity. He was about to hold it up to the light when he realized Mrs. Cosgrove was watching his every movement intently.

"Do you know any more party tricks?"

"Old habits die hard." Monsieur Pamplemousse bent down and held his glass near the floor so that Pommes Frites

108

could share his pleasure. "It is a beautiful wine. I feel highly honored. I only hope my *andouillette* stands comparison by its side. It will have a lot to live up to."

"Aristide?" Mrs. Cosgrove sounded hesitant.

He glanced up at her. *"Oui?"*

"I don't know quite how to put this, but . . . it's just that in England we have a saying—'Two's company, three's a crowd.' What I really mean is, will *he* be watching?"

"Pommes Frites? Watching?" Monsieur Pamplemousse considered the matter. What a strange question.

"It is possible. It depends on his mood."

"All the time? Everything?"

"Of course. He has a very sociable nature. He likes to join in things."

"Oh!" Mrs. Cosgrove sat down in the chair. She seemed depressed by the news. "Oh, dear. I . . . I didn't think you were like that. I mean . . ."

"Don't worry." Monsieur Pamplemousse tried to sound as soothing as possible. "Despite his size he is really a very gentle dog. Normally he wouldn't hurt a fly—not unless he is roused."

"Is he very easily . . . roused?"

"Again, it depends. He has, how would you say?—a strong sense of what is right and what is wrong. If he feels he is being done out of what should be his, then he can get very roused. I would not like to stand in his way at such times. Then, of course, we always share things. If he feels left out then sometimes jealousy sets in."

Mrs. Cosgrove seemed less than reassured by the reply. Having contemplated her glass for a moment or two she suddenly drained it and reached for the bottle.

"Oh, well, *c'est la vie.* In for a penny, in for a pound. When in Rome do as the Romans do."

Monsieur Pamplemousse tried without success to seek the meaning behind these seemingly unconnected remarks. Taken separately they made very little sense; strung together they defied analysis. He wondered if Mrs. Cosgrove was suffering some kind of mental disturbance. She was certainly having a bad attack of the "leg swingings" he'd noticed earlier. Perhaps it was time to get on with the matter in hand. It would be a pity to let such good wine go unaccompanied. He took a firm grip of his stick.

"*Excusez moi.* I must go to the bathroom. We are wasting precious time."

Unaccountably, Mrs. Cosgrove blushed. "It isn't strictly necessary you know. To take precautions, I mean."

"Experience has taught me," said Monsieur Pamplemousse, "that one can never be too careful. I shall not be long." Closing the bathroom door behind him, he bent down and peered inside Pommes Frites's kennel. It was, as always, a model of neatness. The sausages he'd cast through the opening in great haste were now lying in a neat pile at the back. There was almost a military precision about the way they had been arranged, smallest at the front, largest at the rear. *Saucisse de Toulouse* lay beside *Saucisse de Campagne, Saucisson-cervelas* snuggled up against *Saucisson de Bretagne,* but of *andouilles* and *andouillettes* there was not the slightest sign. Paradou must have decided that it was a case of *prudence est mère de sûreté,* and prudence being the better part of valor, he had gone for the nearest.

No matter. Monsieur Pamplemousse put his arm inside the kennel and groped for a likely candidate among the remaining sausages. Perhaps it wasn't meant to be. One should never judge a sausage by its skin, and *andouillettes* could be unpredictable at the best of times; some he'd come across in his travels would have tested the strongest of stomachs. Far better to choose one which would match the wine.

His hand encountered one much larger than the rest, somewhere near the back. A giant of a *saucisson,* he remembered seeing it before and at the time mentally reserving it for a special occasion.

"Sapristi!" He gave a gasp as he lifted it out. At a guess it must weigh all of three kilograms. Enough to keep them all happy for the rest of the evening. And afterward? Afterward, he would let matters take their course.

Clasping the *saucisson* in both hands, he rose to his feet and made for the door. Crooking the little finger of his right hand around the light cord, he gave it a tug, then maneuvered the door handle down with his left arm and gave it a push. The door opened onto more darkness, a darkness made even more impenetrable by his glasses, stretching their photochromatic qualities far beyond anything envisaged by their designers.

"Qu'est-ce que c'est?"

"I hope you don't mind." Mrs. Cosgrove's voice sounded tremulous. "Your world is one of total nighttime, I know. So it will mean nothing to you, but to me it will mean everything. It will make us equal. I have turned out the light."

"As you wish," said Monsieur Pamplemousse unhappily. Life had many strange and unexpected twists—that was part of its richness—but he had to admit that a minute ago he wouldn't have remotely pictured himself groping about in his own room carrying a giant *saucisson.* It would certainly be hard to explain to others. Doucette wouldn't believe him —not in a million years. That apart, he had other, more pressing problems on his mind. He wished now he'd made a more accurate mental note of the positioning of the furniture.

Steering a course as best he could to the right of center, so as to avoid treading on Pommes Frites—assuming Pommes Frites was where he'd left him, he headed in the general direction of the table.

"Merde! Nom d'un nom!"

"Are you all right? Where are you? I can't see you." Mrs. Cosgrove sounded anxious.

"I have stubbed my toe on a leg of the bed." It was

agony. It felt as though it had been broken in at least six places.

"Aaah!" Short though it was, Mrs. Cosgrove managed to imbue the word with a wealth of meaning. A moment later there was a rustle and she was by his side, breathing his name. And each time she breathed his name it was accompanied by a little sob and a wriggle. It was like standing beside a bellydancer who was having trouble with her act.

His heart missed a beat as something gossamer-light landed at his feet and he realized the truth of the matter. At least it answered an earlier question; answered it and immediately posed another.

Like most Capricorns, Monsieur Pamplemousse had a strong sense of priorities. Once a course had been set he didn't like deviating from it. Mentally he had geared himself to satisfying the desires of the inner man before anything else. The message had gone out to all departments; taste buds were throbbing in anticipation, salivary glands were at the ready, the stomach was standing by ready to receive. On the other hand . . .

"Here, take this for a moment." Holding out the *saucisson,* he started to prepare himself for a change of plan.

"Jesus!"

"*Oui, c'est ça.*" It came back to him. "That is its name. *Jésus.*" His opinion of Mrs. Cosgrove went up several more points. She obviously knew her *charcuterie* as well as she knew her *vin rouge.* She would do well on Ananas's quiz show. "It is from the Jura. I am told it is delicious served with *pomme à l'huile.*"

Hovering on one leg as he gingerly removed the sock from his bad foot, Monsieur Pamplemousse suddenly realized he was talking to himself. Mrs. Cosgrove was no longer there. Reaching out, he made contact with her outstretched form on the bed. His reward was a long, drawn-out moan.

"Aristide!" A hand took hold of his and gently but firmly guided it toward the head of the bed. Beneath the silk of the dress her *boîte à lolo* felt warm and inviting. Warm and inviting and . . .

He gave a start. Someone was knocking on the door. Knocking, moreover, in a manner which suggested that whoever was responsible would not readily go away without an answer.

"Un moment." Panic set in as he reached out and turned on the bedside light. For a split second he toyed with the idea of covering Mrs. Cosgrove with the duvet, but one look at her made him change his mind. In her present state of mind there was no knowing how she might react.

A second knock, louder this time and even more insistent, spurred him into action. Reflexes born of years in the Force took over. Putting his arms around Mrs. Cosgrove, he lifted her bodily off the bed and dragged her toward the bathroom. *En route* he essayed a kick at the *saucisson* and immediately wished he hadn't. It was his bad foot. With his other leg he hooked the *culottes* under the bed.

Pommes Frites jumped to his feet and stared at his master in astonishment. He hadn't seen such a furious burst of activity for a long time. It looked a very good game and he hurried around the room collecting all the items in case they were needed for a repeat performance.

"Where are you taking me? What do you want to do with me? Tell me! Tell me!" Brought to her senses at last, Mrs. Cosgrove gazed wildly around the bathroom, first at the pile of sausages on the floor, then at Pommes Frites's kennel.

"Shush!" Monsieur Pamplemousse put a finger to his lips and then planted a kiss on her forehead. "Please. I will explain everything later."

Closing the bathroom door before she had time to answer, he made for the other door just as it started to open. Ananas was waiting outside. He looked furtive, as if he hadn't wanted to be seen there.

"May I come in?"

"I am a little busy. Could it not wait until later?"

"I will not keep you more than a moment or two. What I have to say I would rather say in the privacy of your room."

"As you wish." Monsieur Pamplemousse shrugged. Clearly Ananas had no intention of leaving until he'd had his say. The sooner he got it off his chest and went away again the better.

Ananas took in the bottle and the two glasses, the state of the bed and Monsieur Pamplemousse's foot, but made no comment.

"I have come to tell you that I no longer require your services."

Monsieur Pamplemousse raised his eyebrows. "Really? You mean there is no one trying to blackmail you after all?"

Ananas dismissed the suggestion with a wave of his freshly manicured hand. "Shall we say it was a little misunderstanding all around. The good Herr Schmuck was merely taking precautionary measures to ensure that I would do something I fully intended doing anyway. Château Morgue has been getting some bad press recently and he wants me to restore its respectability. You or I would have done the same thing had we been in his place."

"You might," said Monsieur Pamplemousse gruffly, "I wouldn't."

Ananas inclined his head. "Perhaps. But in the end we all protect that which we believe to be rightfully ours. I admit I might have chosen a different means. However, we all have our methods."

"You mean—you will give him your endorsement—after all that has happened?"

"In return for certain favors—why not? It is a business arrangement."

"You will endorse the work of someone who is prepared to resort to blackmail when it suits him?"

"Blackmail is not a word I like. I prefer the term 'making

an offer it is hard to refuse.' So much more elegant, don't you think? Believe me, if I did not wish to agree to his suggestion I would have carried on with our arrangement. As it is, I would prefer that you forget our previous conversation. We have talked too much already. However, I felt I owed you some kind of explanation and an apology for any unnecessary work you have been put to. Who knows? I may be in a position to do you a favor one day. In the meantime, perhaps you would be kind enough to let me have the photograph back and we will call it a day."

"I'm afraid," said Monsieur Pamplemousse, "that will not be possible."

"Not possible? Don't tell me that after all your moralizing, Pamplemousse, you too have thoughts of straying from the straight and narrow? Because, if so, I warn you that you will find you have picked the wrong person. You will also find that Herr Schmuck does not take kindly to being crossed either."

Monsieur Pamplemousse took a deep breath. Really, the man was totally insufferable. "It is not possible," he said, drawing as much pleasure as he could from the few words, "because the photograph is no longer in my possession. It is in the hands of the police."

"The police!" The remark had its desired effect. Ananas went pale, his normally suave manner deserting him along with his polished accent. "What the devil do you mean by giving it to them?"

"I didn't," said Monsieur Pamplemousse mildly. "They took it. There was a little confusion about the identity of the person playing what one might call the 'leading role.' It is something I still cannot entirely see myself, but . . . as they probably didn't even know you were here at the time, it was understandable."

Ananas relaxed. "I have to admit to sharing your feelings on the subject. It is a cross we have to bear. But," his mind raced ahead of him, "in view of your past reputation, I agree it was an understandable error. People—even members of the police force—have a habit of putting two and two together and coming up with whatever number they choose to fit the bill.

"I would not like to be in your shoes, Pamplemousse. I shall, of course, deny all knowledge of the affair, and in the circumstances I have no doubt the others in the picture will too. They will know on which side their bread is buttered. The negative, no doubt, is still in existence, but now that is your problem."

Ananas pressed home his advantage. "Why are you here anyway? Herr Schmuck would not be pleased if he knew the truth—he would not be pleased at all. An ex-member of the Sûreté, wandering around with a white stick and dark glasses—pretending you have lost your sight, cluttering up the place with that dreadful dog."

"Pommes Frites?" Ignoring the implied threat in the last part of the remark, Monsieur Pamplemousse took a deep breath. He was about to launch himself into the attack when there was a stirring at his feet.

Pommes Frites knew a compliment when he heard one; he was also very sensitive to the reverse side of the coin. Sensing that there was little love lost between his master and Ananas, he'd been keeping a low profile, trying to catch the drift of the conversation, but without much success. He was, despite his fearsome appearance when the occasion demanded, one of nature's mediators.

He'd been considering the matter ever since Ananas first came into the room—watching points, pricking up his ears at changes in the conversation, and he'd come to the conclusion that there was definitely a feeling of acrimony in the air.

What was needed, in his opinion, was some kind of gift. It went against the grain because on the whole he was usually fairly careful in his choice of recipient; he wasn't at all sure that he liked Ananas. In fact, sensitive to the tone of the last remark, he definitely didn't, but if it helped his master in any way, then so be it.

Pommes Frites was a great believer in gifts during moments of crisis. Slippers were his specialty. He often fetched Madame Pamplemousse's slippers if she came in with the shopping on a wet day and saw his paw marks over the floor. It almost always had a soothing effect.

Slippers were obviously out on this occasion, but his eye had caught something else that he felt sure would fill the bill. It looked like a very good present indeed. Reaching out with his paw, he drew the object toward him. Then, feeling very pleased with himself, he courteously offered it to Ananas and stood back to watch the effect. He wasn't disappointed.

A smile spread slowly across Ananas's face as he allowed Mrs. Cosgrove's *culottes* to slip through his fingers, rather like a conjuror about to turn them into a complete set of the flags of all nations.

"Good boy!" Catching them deftly in his other hand, he slipped them into his pocket, then reached down to give Pommes Frites a friendly pat.

Pommes Frites stiffened. From the look on his master's face he could see that he hadn't done the right thing.

Ananas glanced around the room again. "My, we have been having fun, haven't we? Tit, if you will pardon the expression, for tat." He paused with his hand on the door. "No photograph, no present back. *À bientôt.*"

He made to close the door but Monsieur Pamplemousse swiftly intercepted him.

"I imagine you will get your photograph back when the police have finished interviewing the others involved. There is some concern about the state of their health. No doubt they will be in touch in due course."

It was a cheap jibe, but the look on Ananas's face made him feel better.

As he went back into his room the bathroom door

opened and Mrs. Cosgrove appeared. He suddenly felt guilty. In the excitement he'd totally forgotten her presence. But he needn't have worried. Her eyes were shining as she closed the door behind her and came toward him.

He held out his hands to greet her. "I am sorry. I would have told you, sooner or later. Once you start something it is often difficult to go back on it. At least when we last met I was wearing my dark glasses."

Mrs. Cosgrove colored as the truth of the situation came home to her. "Oh! You mean all the time you spent in my room when I was taking a shower . . . Oh dear! What must you have thought?"

"I thought you were very beautiful."

"I don't know what to say."

"Then let us say nothing." Monsieur Pamplemousse suddenly felt a great warmth toward her. It was as if he'd been privileged to know another human being in a way that no one, perhaps not even her husband, had ever done before. It was not to be abused. "Misused words generate misleading thoughts."

He reached for the wine and refilled their glasses. Sadly, it was the end of the bottle. "Let us drink to the future—not the past."

Tilting his glass forward he held it over the white cover of one of the books. "Look at that color. Think of all the love and care and attention that went into making it, and think how lucky we are to be drinking it now."

Mrs. Cosgrove touched his glass momentarily with hers. "I've never met a detective before. At least, not a French one. It's not a bit as I imagined it might be."

"You're not meeting one now. Only an ex-detective."

"I bet you were a very good detective and I don't care what you're doing here just so long as you're not on the side of that odious creature."

"People say we are like each other."

"You are nothing like each other. Only a fool would think that."

He sipped the wine, tasting it properly for the first time. It was round and fruity, at its best, and yet with many years ahead of it still. Full of promise, a wine to be savored and lingered over, not one to be hurried. The analogy between it and the person sitting opposite him was irresistible.

"You must find the negative."

"Pouf! The negative! That doesn't worry me. It is all the other things—things I don't understand."

"Then we must find out about them too. I'll help." Her eyes were sparkling with excitement again. "We'll pool what we know. There are a lot of things I could tell you. Things I've heard. It may be gossip, but you know what they say—where there's smoke there's fire."

Monsieur Pamplemousse hesitated. By nature and by his work with *Le Guide* he had grown unused to working too closely with others. On the other hand . . .

"That would be—very good." He hesitated again. 'Perhaps it is time for the *saucisson* now. If you wish I will turn off the light." He thought he knew the answer as he posed the question and wondered what he would do if he was wrong.

Mrs. Cosgrove shook her head. "I'm not in the right mood anymore."

"They say that appetite comes with eating."

"No, it wouldn't be right somehow. But thank you. Tomorrow perhaps." She stood up. "I know what—tomorrow evening we'll go down to the village. There's a little café. Strictly speaking it's out of bounds, but no one need know. We can work things out over a meal." Pausing at the door, she turned as if she had something else to say. Monsieur Pamplemousse wondered what he would do if she asked for her *culottes* back. Should he tell her the truth, that they were in Ananas's pocket? Or should he save her embarrassment and say he wanted to keep them as a souvenir. Perhaps he could pretend Pommes Frites had hidden them.

"Do you have a car?"

"*Oui.* But not here."

"Can you ride a bike?"

"A *bike?*" He wondered if he was hearing correctly.

"A *bicyclette.* I've got one and I know where I could borrow another for you. How about it?"

Monsieur Pamplemousse considered the matter for all of ten seconds. "They say you never forget. There was a time—"

"Good! *Dors bien!*" Her goodnight kiss, full on the lips, took him by surprise. A moment later she was gone.

"*Dors bien!*" He wondered how much sleep he would get that night.

Pommes Frites looked at him inquiringly and then decided to try his luck again. He reached out a paw. Knowing his master's tastes and adding the fact that it was long past their dinner time, a *saucisson*—even one that was looking slightly the worse for wear through being kicked across the room—was decidedly better than nothing.

7

Dinner for Three

"I'll tell you another thing," said Mrs. Cosgrove. "As far as I can make out, they've all been foreign. Not French, I mean. Mostly Spanish, a few Italians, a couple from South America. Come to think of it, there were no British either. They were all Latins."

"And all with thick calves?"

"You may laugh, but it's true. I've seen enough old dears in my job. When did you last come across anyone that age with that kind of problem?"

Monsieur Pamplemousse fell silent. It was an unanswerable question. He didn't make a habit of going around looking at old ladies' legs.

Mrs. Cosgrove looked anxiously across the table. "I say, are you all right? You haven't hurt yourself?"

"It is nothing. A little soreness. An old wound. It will soon disappear." Slipping his pen between his left leg and the chair seat for safety, Monsieur Pamplemousse waved his other hand reassuringly through the air.

It wasn't a direct lie, merely a slight distortion of the truth. His right leg was certainly sore, but then so was the rest of him. Parts of his body he hadn't been aware of for years were aching. His back, for example. And his neck. Not to mention his *derrière*. His thighs—*mon Dieu!* His thighs felt as though they had been drawn slowly through a mangle, a mangle with rollers made of corrugated iron. As for his own calves, they must be twice their normal size. If his right leg felt worse than the rest of him it was because it had never fully recovered after being peppered by shot from a gun fired at close quarters during a previous assignment.

The truth of the matter was, he'd been trying to make some surreptitious notes on his pad and it wasn't easy. During the gaps in the conversation, his pen had been fairly racing over the pages. Whether he would be able to read his writing was another matter, but the little *bistro* Mrs. Cosgrove had taken him to was a discovery indeed. To the best of his knowledge it had never received a mention in *Le Guide,* nor in any of its competitors. If the smells coming from the kitchen were anything to go by, he was hot on the trail of a very worthwhile entry, possibly Stock Pot material. It would be something of a *coup.* It might even redeem him in the director's eyes for the loss of the letter. From the occasional stirrings and lip smackings emerging from below the folds of the red-and-white checked tablecloth he sensed that Pommes Frites shared his excitement, tempering a growing impatience with anticipation of the good things to come.

"Have you had many wounds? I mean, is what you do often dangerous?"

Monsieur Pamplemousse considered the matter carefully before replying. "The answer to the first question, *touche du bois,* is no. As to the second, it is no more dangerous than what I have just been through."

He spoke with feeling. When Mrs. Cosgrove first suggested cycling down to the village for dinner he'd had a mental picture of setting forth on something fairly sedate; perhaps an old upright that had once belonged to the local *facteur.* In the event she had turned up with an almost brand new British Dawes, complete with a Huret fifteen-speed Dérailleur gear, Italian drop handlebars, and a Dutch all-leather racing saddle. A truly international machine, and one that could have done with a certain amount of adjustment before they set out. The lowering of the saddle, for example. He winced and shifted uneasily in his chair as he recalled the saddle. Heaven alone knew where Mrs. Cosgrove had got hold of the machine. He didn't dare ask.

The first few moments, carrying it through the undergrowth leading to a back way out of the Château, had been bliss. Light as a feather, the very feel of it had brought boyhood memories flooding back. In those days he had owned an André Bertin, and conversation had been all about the relative merits of wooden as opposed to alloy wheel rims; of brazed versus welded frames.

Once outside Château Morgue, though, it had been a very different story. In the far off days of his youth he had barely touched sixty kilos on the scales—the optimum weight the designers of his present machine must have had in mind. The roads, too, had been much smoother, the hairpin bends more suitably cambered, of that he was sure. Seen at close quarters, the road from Château Morgue down to the village had been one *nid de poule* after another. "Hen nests" was an understatement for such potholes. He hadn't felt quite so frightened for a long time. He now knew from personal experience how Pommes Frites must feel every time he set off head-first down a flight of stairs. Except that with stairs the end was usually in sight. The journey down to the village had seemed neverending.

Mrs. Cosgrove, on the other hand, had taken it all in her stride. Eschewing the added protection of layers of material between her *derrière* and the saddle, she'd actually lifted her skirt over the top, allowing it to drape down either side in a most provocative manner as she led the way down the hill. At any other time and under other circumstances, he would have found the sight more than a little disturbing. Instead of which he'd spent most of the time holding onto the handlebars like grim death, hardly daring to change gear lest he got into an uncontrollable wobble or, worse still, collided with Pommes Frites, who treated the whole thing as yet another new game, running on ahead and waiting in the middle of the road for his master to appear, leaving it until the last possible moment to leap to one side.

To add to his ignominious arrival in the village, Mrs. Cosgrove had greeted him rather like the last rider home in the *Tour de France,* tying onto his handlebars a large, plastic, helium-filled balloon that she'd found in a local shop, by way of consolation.

He glanced around the restaurant. There were only seven tables, two of which were already occupied by regulars. Above a pine-wood fire in a large open grate was an old-fashioned spit—a complicated arrangement of weights and pulleys—the like of which he hadn't seen for a long time. It looked as though it was still in regular use. No doubt if you ordered a steak during the summer months there would be a girl whose job it was to lay the firewood in exactly the right way, not too little, not too much, so that the meat would be cooked just as the chef thought it should be—take it or leave it.

To be true, the menu was short—again take it or leave it, but from the moment they took their seats and a plate of almond and aniseed-flavored biscuits, fresh from the oven, was plonked on their table, automatically and without comment, he knew that he was dealing with the genuine article; a chef who definitely liked his food. Moreover, from the glimpses he'd caught through the serving hatch separating the kitchen from the dining room, a satisfactorily rotund chef. On the whole he tended to mistrust thin chefs, classing them alongside bald-headed barbers who tried to sell you bottles of hair restorer. Neither were any advertisement for their trade.

The *patron*'s wife, who took the orders in between sitting at her cash desk near the door, was by contrast thin-lipped and forbidding. It was a classic combination. The man happy in his kitchen. The wife out front looking after the money.

"I'm sorry. It's not very exciting." Mrs. Cosgrove looked genuinely disappointed as she scanned the handwritten menu. "But it makes a change."

"Not exciting!" Monsieur Pamplemousse gazed at her. "It is the most exciting menu I have seen for a long time. Here you will find food of a kind you will get nowhere else in France. Why? Because the chef has probably never been farther than Narbonne in his life. He knows no other *cuisine,* and even if he did he wouldn't admit to it."

He pushed the plate of biscuits toward her, at the same time signaling to the Madame. "Have another *resquille.* We will do them the compliment of helping them on their way with a bottle of Blanquette de Limoux—if they have one. It is a local sparkling wine. Not quite like the real thing perhaps, but I think you will like it."

He ran a practiced eye down the menu. "Then I suggest you try the *cargolade—escargots* grilled over vinestocks; it gives them a unique flavor. I will have mine *à la Languedocienne*—with a sauce of anchovies, ham, cognac, and walnuts. We can share with each other."

To his pleasure the Blanquette de Limoux more than fulfilled the promise he'd made, adding to the healthy glow of Mrs. Cosgrove's cheeks; a glow further enhanced by the soft light from a single candle on their table. Taking advantage of the moment he made another note on his pad. The wine had the smell of cider characteristic of the Mauzac grape which was its main ingredient, but there was another element he couldn't quite place. Perhaps the addition of some Chardonnay. He'd read somewhere that the best *cuvées* used it to give fuller flavor.

Conscious of Mrs. Cosgrove's eyes on him, he returned

to the task in hand. "Have you ever tried *Brandade de Morue?*"

Mrs. Cosgrove shook her head. "I've heard of it."

"Then that is a must. Dried salt cod pounded with garlic and olive oil until it becomes a creamy paste. Then it is served on *croûtons.* Salt cod is their winter equivalent of bacon and salt pork.

"After that, since we are in Catalan country, we could try *Tranche de Mouton à la Catalane,* or *Poivrons Rouges à la Catalane*—red peppers stuffed with rice salad. Again, perhaps we can have a little of each and share. With that we can have a bottle of Côtes de Roussillon Villages—if this wine is anything to go by the *patron* will most likely know a small grower. It could be something special."

He felt in his element. It was like composing a piece of music; a matter of rhythms, of trying to avoid striking a discordant note.

"We could finish off sharing some *Roquefort* over the rest of the wine."

"We seem to be doing a lot of sharing this evening," said Mrs. Cosgrove meaningfully. "First the *escargots,* then the main course, now the *Roquefort.*"

Monsieur Pamplemousse looked up from the menu. She was back into her leg-swinging syndrome. He hoped Pommes Frites was keeping a watchful eye on things below stairs. If she carried on at her present rate he could suffer a nasty blow to the head. He would not be best pleased.

Perhaps it was a good thing they weren't having Chambertin with the cheese. What was it Casanova had said about *Roquefort* and Chambertin being excellent bedfellows? "They stimulate romance and bring budding love affairs to a quick fruition."

He voiced his thoughts and then immediately wished he hadn't. Mrs. Cosgrove was doing well enough with the Blanquette de Limoux on its own. Pommes Frites stirred nervously at his feet.

"George swears by cinnamon. He has it a lot on toast. He always says it puts lead in his pencil."

The mention of the word pencil reminded Monsieur Pamplemousse of his pen which was now balanced very precariously on the edge of the seat. Apart from posing an additional hazard to Pommes Frites's head, he shuddered to think what would happen to its finely engineered tip if it landed on the tiled floor. It would be like losing an extension to his right arm. No other pen would ever be quite the same.

Cautiously he reached down below the cloth and as ill luck would have it made contact with a knee which was palpably not his own.

The sigh of contentment which escaped Mrs. Cosgrove's lips coincided with the arrival of the *escargots*. Madame, her lips more tightly compressed than ever, banged the plates down in front of them, punctuating her action with a loud sniff before retiring to her cash desk.

Feeling aggrieved that his action had been misinterpreted on all fronts, Monsieur Pamplemousse seized the opportunity to withdraw his hand.

"Du pain, s'il vous plaît."

There was another bang as the basket of bread landed on their table.

Mrs. Cosgrove giggled. "You're just like George. He gets put out when things like that happen." Her leg stopped swinging and with one swift pincer movement came together with its opposite number to embrace his own right leg in a vicelike grip. Simultaneously, she reached out and clasped his left hand firmly in hers. It was like having dinner with an octopus. "George likes his greens too!"

"Greens? *Qu'est-ce que ces greens?"*

"Oats. You know . . . dipping his wick."

Monsieur Pamplemousse didn't know, although he could guess. He wondered what Doucette would say if he arrived home one day and announced that he wanted to *plonger* his *mèche de lampe.* He withdrew the thought immediately.

His thoughts went out instead to the absent George. If Mrs. Cosgrove's present behavior was typical of their life together, his free time must be almost entirely taken up with a search for fresh stimulants. Perhaps he wasn't as old as he looked in the photograph. It really was *incroyable* the way the English gave strange names to anything that had the faintest whiff of guilt about it. They seemed to have invented an entire language to cover every eventuality. It was the same with food. They didn't eat, they "noshed," "scoffed," or had "bites" to satisfy the "inner man" or because they felt "peckish," and they followed the main course with large helpings of "pud" which they called "afters."

Perhaps it had to do with being separated from their parents at an early age and the segregation of the sexes. He'd read that it still went on.

Trying to erase from his mind the vision of a dormitory full of little Mrs. Cosgroves, all sitting on the sides of their beds swinging their legs to and fro in a demonstration of mass frustration, he wiped the earthenware dish clean with a piece of bread and passed it down to Pommes Frites.

The *escargots* had been delicious. It was no wonder they were known as "the oysters of Burgundy." Although these, from the vineyards of the Languedoc, were smaller, they were no less good. Catching sight of the *patron* watching him through the serving hatch, he gave the universal, rounded forefinger-to-thumb sign of approval and received a smile in return.

Over the main course he decided to bring the conversation around to more important matters. "So what else can you tell me about Château Morgue? How about the Schmucks?"

"Herr Schmuck comes from Leipzig and is a bit of a mystery. He started out as an industrial chemist, but the middle part of his life is a bit of an enigma. According to the locals he just seemed to materialize one day. Where his wife comes from no one seems to know. She keeps herself very much to herself. I've got a theory she's escaping from something in her past. She goes on a lot of trips, but always by herself."

Monsieur Pamplemousse looked at her curiously as he poured the wine, "How do you know all these things?"

"People unburden themselves when they're having a manicure. You'd be surprised. They talk about the most amazing things. It's a bit like being on a psychiatrist's couch without the guilt feelings afterward."

"And Doctor Furze?"

"He was born in Leipzig too, but he escaped from East Germany just after the war. He's no more a doctor than I am. At least, not a doctor of medicine, which is what he would like everyone to believe."

Feeling a nudge from below, Monsieur Pamplemousse speared a generous portion of *Tranche de Mouton* and passed it down. Since they would both be smelling of garlic that night there was no point in being parsimonious. All the same, he made a mental note to leave the bedroom window open.

The Côtes de Roussillon was young and fruity, not unlike a Châteauneuf du Pape, but softer and more rounded. Casanova might not have ascribed to it quite the same powers as a Chambertin, but it showed up well against the *Roquefort*. And Mrs. Cosgrove too. Her eyes seemed to have acquired an added sparkle.

His brief exchange with the *patron* brought its benefit. With a *Crème d'Homère*—the local version of *crème caramel*, but made with the addition of wine and honey, there came a glass of Muscat from Frontignan, with the compliments of the chef. Golden and honey-scented like the dessert, it made a perfect ending to the meal.

Monsieur Pamplemousse felt a great sense of well-being. A well-being threatened only by a faint but persistent unease in the middle of his chest. It had probably been brought on by overexercise; it certainly couldn't have been the food. It confirmed a theory he'd once seen propounded by an English author whose name he couldn't pronounce, that the body was filled with numerous tiny compartments full of poisonous liquids, all of which lived perfectly happily alongside each other provided they were left in peace. But if you disturbed them by running, jumping, jogging or other unnatural pursuits, then you did so at your peril. Once the fluids were mixed together the result could be fatal.

"Is anything the matter, Aristide?" Mrs. Cosgrove reached for his hand again. "Are you sure you are all right?"

He returned the squeeze while massaging his chest in a circular movement with his other hand. "It will pass. A slight rebellion within, that is all. I should have taken some fresh carrot juice before we came out." Carrot juice ought to have been practically on tap in an establishment like Château Morgue.

"I have a bottle of something back in my room," said Mrs. Cosgrove. "It is made by some monks in the Rhône Valley and it's supposed to be good for the digestion."

Monsieur Pamplemousse declined the offer. Without wishing to appear ungrateful, he had a feeling that what was good for a monk's digestion would probably have little effect on his own after all they had eaten. In his experience monasteries were usually run on strictly business lines by Abbots with clipboards. Miracles were not on sale to the general public.

"Perhaps a little *digestif*?" he added, leaving his options open. Mrs. Cosgrove brightened.

Reminding the Madame of a doggy bag he'd ordered for Pommes Frites when they first arrived, he asked at the same time for the bill, only too well aware of the fact that food was not the only problem. It had been a mistake to order a second bottle of the Côtes de Roussillon.

The bill paid, he rose from the table, adjusted his dark glasses, took hold of Pommes Frites's plastic doggy bag in the same hand as the white stick and, after a suitable exchange of pleasantries all around, led the way by a roundabout route to the door.

"I feel very wibbley-woo," said Mrs. Cosgrove, when they were outside.

Wibbley-woo was not the word for it. On the other hand it wasn't a bad description. Better than *joie-de-vivre*. It even lent itself to variations. Wobbley-wib . . . libbley loo. He decided to make a note of it. Perhaps the English had a point after all. There was a name for everything. It was even possible to sing it. The sound of wibbley-woo echoing back from the stone buildings had a satisfying ring.

The doggy bag safely secured beneath a large clip on the carrier over the rear wheel of his bicycle, Monsieur Pamplemousse removed the balloon from the handlebars and with due solemnity attached it to Pommes Frites's collar.

Mounting the machine, even with the aid of the white stick, was something else again. As he picked himself up for the third time he felt rather than saw someone watching him, and turned to see a pair of eyes through a gap in the curtains of the bistro. They were disapproving eyes, eyes that went well with the thinly compressed mouth, as chilly and unsmiling as the night air. The owner of both was not amused.

Turning his back on the uninvited audience, he picked up the bicycle and pushed it a little way down the road before making another attempt. This time he was more successful.

"Follow me!" Mrs. Cosgrove, skirts flying, was already negotiating a corner ahead of him.

He set off in pursuit. A *pharmacie,* its windows full of large stone jars and photographic equipment, merged with a *boulangerie,* and that gave way to a *bureau de tabac,* which in turn became the souvenir shop where Mrs. Cosgrove had bought the balloon. He wondered if the owners were watching Pommes Frites from their bedroom window.

Filled with an elation brought on by a heady mixture of wine and cold air, he discovered a new courage. Suddenly, he felt confident enough to sit upright in the saddle, holding on to the handlebars, first with only one hand, then with no hands at all.

Obeying a sudden impulse, he went round the *Mairie* a second time. As he shot past the bistro he caught sight of the Madame again and waved his stick at her. His salute was not returned. She was standing beside the cash desk engaged in an earnest conversation on the telephone. He felt her eyes following him.

Soon he was out of the village and heading back toward Château Morgue. Almost immediately the road began to climb. Flushed with success, he went through all fifteen gears with an aplomb he hadn't felt in years, and then came to an abrupt halt as he tried for the sixteenth and found it wasn't there. Looking back over his shoulder he saw to his disappointment that despite everything he had barely covered a hundred meters.

Dismounting, he turned a corner and caught sight of a bicycle lying abandoned at the side of the road near the entrance to the *aire de pique-nique.* Above the wall, ghostlike and silvery in the moonlight, floated the balloon, and beyond that, stretched out on one of the tables, lay Mrs. Cosgrove. Arms locked behind her head, knees drawn up, hair streaming over the edge, she looked for all the world like a reincarnation of Aphrodite resting while gaining her second wind after her long swim in the Mediterranean.

As he laid his own bicycle gently alongside the other, Monsieur Pamplemousse felt his pulse begin to quicken and a watery sensation in the bottom of his stomach. It was a feeling which, as he bent down to remove his cycle clips, was replaced almost immediately by a sharp, stabbing pain higher up.

"Merde!" What a moment to get indigestion.

He was about to straighten up when he heard a long, drawn-out animal grunt coming from somewhere close at hand. It was a complex, elemental sound, accompanied by a kind of snuffling and with overtones of such ferocity it caused him to think twice about removing his clips and to take a firm grip of his stick instead.

Pommes Frites had evidently heard it too, for the balloon was bobbing up and down as if caught in a sudden gust of wind, heading first one way and then the other. Monsieur Pamplemousse turned toward a black patch of undergrowth beneath some trees on the other side of the road, wondering if perhaps it was harboring a wild boar. As he did so the sound came again, this time from behind. He spun around as fast as he could and immediately regretted it. Part of his head felt as if it had gone into orbit. On the other hand, he had identified the source. Unmistakably, the dying notes came from the direction of the table. Mrs. Cosgrove was enjoying a deep if not exactly soundless sleep.

From somewhere in the distance, farther down the hill, there came the roar of engines. By the sound of it two vehicles were approaching fast, their tires squealing as they took the corners at top speed. Monsieur Pamplemousse felt glad he was no longer on his bicycle. The impression that there was more than one vehicle was confirmed a few seconds later as two sets of headlights swung around a bend immediately before the village and then disappeared from view.

Instinct told him to hide. Calling for Pommes Frites to follow, he made a dive for the cover of an old workman's hut in the far corner of the picnic area. It was too late to do anything about Mrs. Cosgrove or the bicycles even if he'd wanted to. They weren't a moment too soon. He'd hardly had time to draw breath, let alone make himself comfortable, before the lights swept past, illuminating as they did so both Mrs. Cosgrove and Pommes Frites's balloon, which had broken free.

There was a screech of brakes from the leading vehicle, echoed even more urgently by the one behind, then the noise of crunching gears and engines revving as they backed down the hill a little before coming to a stop. Doors slammed as the occupants clambered out. Then came the crunch of feet on gravel, followed by the sound of familiar voices.

"It must be the woman the old girl in the café was talking about on the phone." He recognized Paradou's voice, then that of his colleague as they shone a torch over the recumbent figure on the table. There were a few barely suppressed whistles, then the other *gendarme* passed a remark that provoked a coarse laugh. It was immediately stifled as another voice cut through the darkness.

Peering around the side of the hut, Monsieur Pamplemousse saw Inspector Chambard rise into view from behind the bicycles. "Can't you wake her?"

"You try, Chief." It was the second *gendarme*. "She's out like a light."

Chambard gave an impatient grunt. He crossed to the parapet and gazed up at the balloon drifting slowly across the valley. "What the devil can have happened to Pamplemousse? It must have been him. There can't be anyone else wandering around with a white stick at this time of night."

"I wouldn't fancy his chances if he's fallen down there." Paradou joined the inspector and waved his torch in a desultory fashion over the side of the wall.

"Zut alors!" Inspector Chambard turned back to the table and gazed down at Mrs. Cosgrove. "We can't leave her

here. She'll catch her death of cold. You two had better take her back to the station. Put the bicycles in the van too. There's a bag of something on Pamplemousse's carrier— you can go through it when you get back, Paradou, and make a list of the contents."

Paradou gave Pommes Frites's doggy bag a tentative squeeze. "Why do I always get the dirty jobs, Chief?"

But Inspector Chambard was already in his car. The door slammed. A moment later he was on his way. Paradou waited until the car was safely around the corner before giving vent to his feelings.

"You can tell it belongs to old Pamplemousse all right. He must have some kind of kink. Feel it, go on, feel it!"

Declining the offer, his colleague picked up the other bicycle and propped it up in the back of the van. "Did you see the analyst's report on the first lot? Sixty percent pure chicken and pork. Fifteen per cent pure onion—"

"Pure! That's a laugh. Wait till he gets hold of this!"

The second machine safely stowed away, they turned their attention to Mrs. Cosgrove.

From his position behind the bush, a position which was growing steadily more uncomfortable with every passing moment, it seemed to Monsieur Pamplemousse that the two *gendarmes* were making unnecessarily heavy weather of the comparatively simple task of transferring their burden from the table to the front seat of the van.

The temptation to jump out and remonstrate was almost too great to bear, but discretion won the day. He was in no mood to submit to the kind of tedious explanations that would inevitably follow such an action. Far better let things take their course.

At last they had finished. As the red tail lights of the van receded down the hill, Monsieur Pamplemousse stood up and mopped his brow with the back of his sleeve. In spite of the cold he was sweating profusely.

He turned and gazed up the hill toward Château Morgue.

The lights from the windows at the top of the tower block made it seem even more remote and impregnable than ever, and he suddenly felt very dispirited. It would need either the services of a helicopter pilot to learn what was going on inside or a bird perched on top of Pommes Frites's balloon.

Saddle sore, aching in every limb, his gastric juices in revolt, head throbbing, deprived of his sole means of wheeled transport, Monsieur Pamplemousse prepared himself for the long slog back up the hill.

Only one thing remained to render his cup of unhappiness full to overflowing. It concerned Pommes Frites and was a matter that would need to be faced up to in the not too distant future.

For the moment at least, Pommes Frites had other things on his mind. He was standing with his front paws on the parapet looking for his lost balloon, but when he mentally came back down to earth it would be with a distinct bump. He wouldn't be best pleased when it dawned on him that along with Mrs. Cosgrove and the bicycles had gone the bag containing his supper. He would feel very hard done by. Melancholy would set in. And when Pommes Frites had a touch of the melancholics, everyone else was apt to suffer. It was not a happy prospect.

"Merde!" Monsieur Pamplemousse picked up his stick and stabbed at a nearby bush. What a way to end an evening that had begun with such promise.

8

Journey into Space

Contrary to all his expectations, Monsieur Pamplemousse went to sleep that night almost as soon as his head touched the pillow. He woke at eight o'clock the next morning feeling, if not as fresh as the proverbial daisy, at least as a daisy which required the minimum amount of attention in order to greet the new day. After a bath and a shave and a hearty breakfast of *Saucisses de Montbéliard,* he felt more than ready to start work.

To say that he spent the intervening time thinking of Mrs. Cosgrove would have been a distortion of the truth. She entered his mind more than once, but only in passing. At least he knew she was in safe hands, and doubtless she would surface again in the fullness of time.

His mind was full of little notes and observations and thoughts, all of which badly needed putting into some kind of order. In many ways it was the part he liked best, the sifting of all the available information, the analyzing, collating, and fitting together of all the various items like a jigsaw puzzle, discarding a piece here, adding a piece there, watching the overall picture gradually take shape. There was a precision about the whole activity; the knowledge that an answer must eventually be produced appealed to the mathematical side of his mind. True, in the present case there were a number of bits missing, but he had no doubt in his mind that once he'd got the edge pieces assembled, the framework and parameters within which he had to work established, the rest would follow.

With no thought of time or of Pommes Frites, he worked solidly for the best part of an hour, then he laid down his pen and sat for a while, driven to one inescapable conclusion. Whichever way he looked at it, from whatever direction he approached the problem, in order to prove his theory he needed evidence of what went on inside the Tower Block. He rose and crossed to the window, gazing out at the surrounding countryside, going over in his mind once again all that had taken place since his arrival at Château Morgue. And as had so often happened in the past when, under similar circumstances, he'd sought inspiration from the waters of the Seine via his office window in the *quai des Orfèvres,* the very act of stretching his legs and filling his mind with an entirely different view, produced almost immediate results.

By standing on tiptoe he could just see the village where he had spent the previous evening with Mrs. Cosgrove; by standing on a chair he could even see the *aire de pique-nique,* and it was while he was idly wondering what had happened to Pommes Frites's balloon, whether it was somewhere inland, or perhaps even heading toward the Mediterranean, that an idea came to him.

He stood on the chair for a moment or two, lost in thought. It would require equipment he didn't possess, equipment he probably couldn't easily get hold of at short notice. Unless . . . In a flash, one idea triggered off another. He looked at his watch. Ten o'clock. Jumping down off the chair he made for the bathroom, and, watched by Pommes Frites, set to work.

At 10:13, unable to stand things a moment longer,

138

Pommes Frites made it very clear that he wished to be elsewhere. He left the room with a worried look on his face and set off down the corridor, determined to brook no interference with his plans.

Monsieur Pamplemousse wasn't the only one to have spent his morning engaged in thought. Pommes Frites had also been exercising his gray matter, and after weighing up all the pros and cons, making all due allowances for possible errors of judgment, it was his considered opinion that his master was suffering some kind of brainstorm and that there wasn't a moment to be lost.

The signs were all there. First, there had been the business with the white stick and dark glasses; then the sudden change of eating habits—from meals of infinite variety to a diet of unrelieved sausages. The acquisition of a bicycle was yet another bad sign. Pommes Frites didn't agree with bicycles—they came at you from all angles. As for the balloon, the less said the better. The fact that his master was now playing around with his kennel was the final straw. It suggested that action of an immediate and fundamental nature was required.

No less adept, although perhaps a trifle slower than his master at sifting information, it had taken Pommes Frites some while to arrive at the truth of the matter. Now that he had, he couldn't understand why it hadn't occurred to him before. The whole thing was his fault entirely. His master was in need of care and attention and in his hour of need he, Pommes Frites, had been responsible, albeit unwittingly, for giving away something that he obviously held in great store. It was as if, and he couldn't think of a better parallel, it was as if someone had stumbled across a store of his best bones and had given them to another dog without so much as a by-your-leave.

Pommes Frites was never one for doing things by halves. Once he had things clearly worked out in his mind, that was that—there was no stopping him. And had he been able to see his master at that moment, he would undoubtedly have quickened his pace toward his final goal, for his worst fears would have been realized.

Monsieur Pamplemousse, with the aid of a puncture repair kit normally housed in a pocket at the rear of Pommes Frites's kennel, was busily engaged in gluing down the flap over the entrance, and in so doing, effectively barring the way at one and the same time to both anyone who might seek entry and anything within hoping to escape, including, he was pleased to see as he applied his full weight to the top and bounced up and down several times, the air inside.

Pommes Frites would not have been alone in registering concern had there been others present to witness the operation, but Monsieur Pamplemousse himself seemed more than pleased as he gazed at the result of his labors; so much so it was some little while before he registered the fact that the telephone was ringing.

"Aristide." It was Mrs. Cosgrove.

"Anne. How are you?"

"I feel awful."

Monsieur Pamplemousse felt his forehead. "I am not . . . how would you say? One hundred percent, but—"

"I don't mean that. I mean the whole thing. It's never happened to me before. I'm fine otherwise."

Monsieur Pamplemousse decided to try again, rephrasing his original question. *"Where* are you?"

"I'm still at the police station. Some inspector or other has been questioning me. He says he knows you."

"Chambard?"

"That's the one. He thought you were with me last night. Apparently the woman in the restaurant gave him a description. I didn't let on. I said I was with your look-alike. The one who came to your room that night."

"Ananas?" He felt his forehead again. The dizziness had returned. "Ananas!"

"I don't think he quite believed me at first because of

your white stick. Anyway, he does now. I didn't want to get you involved in case you wanted to keep a low profile."

"It is very kind of you." Monsieur Pamplemousse hesitated. For some totally illogical reason he felt slightly put out that his place had been taken, if only on paper as it were, by someone he disliked so much.

"You don't mind?" She sounded anxious.

"Of course not. I am a little jealous, that is all."

"Oh dear. I'm sorry about that. Never mind. We'll try and make up for it later. I'll tell you something else—"

"Listen, before you do . . ." Monsieur Pamplemousse cut across whatever Mrs. Cosgrove had been about to say. Her telephone call was opportune. An omen, perhaps, that what he was planning was meant. He wondered if their conversation was being overheard, and then decided to take the risk. It was too good a chance to miss. "On your way back you can do some shopping for me. I would like you to stop off in the village and go, first of all, to the souvenir shop, the one where you bought the balloon. Then I would like you to go to the *pharmacie*. I think you will find the owner is a keen photographer. I need a number of things. I saw most of them in the window last night. You had better make a list."

While he was talking, Monsieur Pamplemousse found himself marveling at the wonders of the human brain, able to register and retain even the most trivial details without being prompted, and all at a time when it must have been heavily engaged in supplying information to that section which was making sure he remained safely upright on his bicycle. He could still picture the window display in the *pharmacie* with the utmost clarity.

"Have you got all that?"

"I think so. Would you like me to read it back?"

"Not if you are sure." At this stage he did not wish to arouse Chambard's interest in his activities any more than it was already. For the time being at least, he would rather work on his own. Just himself and Pommes Frites . . . and Mrs. Cosgrove. Chambard was a good man, but he would be bound to ask questions. If his own theories proved correct there would soon be plenty of need for his services.

"Before you go, I must tell you. There have been some more goings-on at the Château."

"Goings-on?"

"Someone's been through the ladies' changing rooms like a dose of salts." Mrs. Cosgrove's voice became muffled as she put a hand over her mouth, covering up a half-suppressed giggle. "Apparently they all came back from their morning saunas and needle baths and found their most precious items of underwear missing. There's hell to pay. Inspector Chambard's on the phone about it right now. That's how I could ring you. He thinks it must be the same person who stole the package a couple of days ago. He says—"

Monsieur Pamplemousse looked at his watch again. Much as he liked the sound of Mrs. Cosgrove's voice, it was 10:43 and time was precious. He had a great deal to do.

"I can tell you one thing, and I will stake my reputation on it. Whoever was responsible for taking the *charcuterie* is in no way involved in the present matter." He was about to add, "And you can tell Inspector Chambard that from me!," but thought better of it. Conscious that he might have sounded a trifle pompous, he ended on a fonder note.

"Take care. I hope I will see you soon."

At 10:45, just as he was in the act of laying out his camera equipment on the bed for checking, there was a loud thump on the door. He opened it and Pommes Frites staggered in. At least, he assumed it was Pommes Frites; it was hard to tell beneath the vast mound of multicolored material he was holding in his mouth.

With all the aplomb of an elderly magician whose *pièce de résistance,* the trick he keeps for really special occasions—

that of the disappearing *culottes* of all nations—has gone sadly awry, he came to a halt in the middle of the room and disgorged his load over the rug.

Suffering a feeling of *déjà vu,* Monsieur Pamplemousse shot a quick look up and down the corridor. Somewhere in the distance an alarm bell was ringing, but otherwise all was quiet. He closed the door and gazed unhappily at the pile of *lingerie.* Although black undoubtedly held pride of place, with white a close second, *culottes* of red, green, purple, and blue, all the many colors of the rainbow, manifested themselves in a variety of shapes, sizes, and degrees of laciness. At a cursory glance, if sheer weight of numbers was any criterion, Pommes Frites's latest excursion into the world of fashion had been even more successful than his earlier venture into the more mundane realms of *charcuterie.*

Well pleased with his morning's work, Pommes Frites stretched, and wagged his tail in anticipation of the words of praise to come. Although his master seemed temporarily bereft of speech, he was prepared to wait, happy in the knowledge that he had done the right thing at last. It had just been a simple case of good intentions gone wrong. Mrs. Cosgrove had removed an article of clothing, intending it as a gift for Monsieur Pamplemousse, and he, Pommes Frites, had presented it to another. No wonder his master had been upset; small wonder, too, that he now looked so bowled over at his good fortune—it called for some more tail wagging.

Monsieur Pamplemousse stared back at Pommes Frites through eyes glazed not by tears, but with sheer incredulity. He couldn't bring himself to say *"bon garçon"* his lips refused to form the words. On the other hand, he couldn't in fairness chastise him either. There was also the fact that he would need Pommes Frites's cooperation later that day and he couldn't afford to let any other misunderstandings come between them.

143

Slowly and deliberately he knelt down and began folding the garments into a neat pile. Compressing them as tightly as possible, he opened the cupboard, emptied the remains of the sausages from their wrapping paper, and used it to make a new parcel which he then pushed under the bed.

It represented yet another very good reason why he would need to work quickly. It was more than likely that Inspector Chambard would seize the opportunity to pay a return visit to Château Morgue. He was not one to be balked. No stone would be left unturned in his search for the culprit; probably no *culottes* either if Paradou had any say in the matter. The prospect of being confronted by innumerable irate ladies seeking to identify their nether garments was not a happy one. Even worse, he would be hard put to it to avoid a second request from the inspector to accompany him back to the station.

He looked out of the window to see if there was any sign of Mrs. Cosgrove returning and was just in time to see the Mercedes in which he'd arrived enter the gates. It was being towed by a breakdown lorry driven by a mechanic in blue overalls. There was no sign of the original chauffeur. The car appeared to have been in the wars since he'd last seen it. The windscreen was smashed, the front bumper twisted, and there was a sizable dent in the radiator.

The morning was clear and sunny, and he was about to open the window to let in some fresh air when his attention was caught by the pole over the main entrance. For the second time since his arrival the flag was flying at half mast. Had his determination that it was time for action shown any signs of wavering, this was enough to give it a boost; as it was, it simply strengthened his resolve.

First there was the camera equipment to check. On his way back to the bed he closed the bathroom door. For the moment at least, he would rather Pommes Frites didn't see his kennel.

Opening up the case belonging to *Le Guide,* he lifted out

the tray containing the camera equipment. Removing the Leica R4 body, the standard fifty millimeter Summicron lens and the motor winder, he began to assemble them. The motor winder responded immediately when he tested it. Loading the camera with Ilford XP1 black-and-white film, he set the program for shutter priority at a speed of one two hundred and fiftieth of a second, and focused the lens at around ten yards. The combination of a lens aperture of f2 and a film speed of four hundred ASA should be sufficient to cover any eventuality. If not, Trigaux back at headquarters would have means of pushing the film beyond its normal rating.

Opening up his own case, he looked for the Remote Control Unit. Once again fate seemed to have stepped in to take a hand. It was the first time he had ever had such a thing with him. Luckily he'd taken Rabillier's advice and included several lengths of extension cable. It would enable him to keep hold of the unit itself and judge to a nicety when to trigger the automatic winder. With a range of anything between one frame every half second and one frame every ten seconds he ought to be able to arrive at a satisfactory optimum rate of exposure.

He would need to reconnoiter the area first and make a rough measurement of the distance along the outside wall of the Tower Block, dividing it by the total number of frames available, to gauge the exposure pattern. Even then it might result in a few blank frames—shots of the wall—but given the total window area he should be all right.

He would probably only have time for one go. There was no sense in pushing his luck, so it would have to be right first time. In the interest of safety, Pommes Frites's kennel had been made of a bright orange, light-reflecting material and would therefore be plainly visible to anyone who happened to be looking out of the windows. Unless . . . He had another flash of inspiration. Unless it was covered in something that didn't reflect the light.

He felt under the bed. Covered with a suitably black, nonreflecting material, it wouldn't be any problem at all.

Pommes Frites wasn't normally given to audible expressions of pleasure. He was content to leave such displays of emotion to creatures of a lower order. But anyone who didn't know him well might have been forgiven had they assumed he was undergoing some strange metamorphosis of a feline and contagious nature as he watched his master undo the parcel. Contagious, because it speedily communicated itself to Monsieur Pamplemousse. Monsieur Pamplemousse was positively purring with delight. Had he been conducting a market survey for a fashion designer who wished to prove that despite all the efforts of his rivals to dictate otherwise, black remained the most popular color in ladies' *lingerie,* he couldn't have wished for better or more unimpeachable proof. Perhaps it had to do with the environment at Château Morgue. Perhaps many of the clients came there not so much for "the cure" as for less laudable reasons. No matter, the plain fact was that he had more than enough material to cover a dozen kennels. Selecting several items that must have belonged to those who had benefited most from nature's generosity, and rejecting others that would have barely covered the air valve, Monsieur Pamplemousse made a fresh but smaller parcel of the ones that had failed to meet his requirements, and replaced it under the bed.

"So it *was* you after all!" At the sound of Mrs. Cosgrove's voice he jumped to his feet, coloring up like a schoolboy caught hiding something untoward beneath his desk lid. He had been concentrating so hard on the task in hand he'd totally failed to hear her enter the room. She looked deflated, like someone whose last precious illusion had just been shattered.

"It was true earlier on when I spoke to you on the phone. Now, I am afraid it is no longer so. On the other hand, *après la pluie, le beau temps."* He picked up the nearest garment and ran it through his fingers, "Every cloud has a silver lining. They solve a problem." To his relief she seemed to accept this without question. It showed on her face.

"You managed to get all the things I asked for?"

Mrs. Cosgrove felt inside a carrier bag. "I have some of them in here, the chemicals, some plaited nylon line. I got extra strong. It has a breaking point of over five kilograms. I hope I did the right thing, but not knowing what you wanted it for . . ."

Briefly and succinctly, Monsieur Pamplemousse ran through his plan. At the same time he made some quick mental calculations. The camera and the lens together weighed something like nine hundred grams, the winder another four hundred. Filled with gas, the kennel should provide more than enough lift.

"The rest of the things are in my room. All except the helium cylinder. That weighs a ton and it will need the two of us. I left it in the rented car."

"Which is where?"

"I parked it out of sight. It's well off the beaten track. I don't think anyone will find it unless they come across it by accident."

"Excellent. I can't thank you enough." Now that things were starting to happen he felt relaxed. His mood communicated itself to Mrs. Cosgrove.

"What are you doing for the rest of the day?"

He hesitated. "Working." It was an understatement. There were measurements to be taken, calculations to be made. He would need to experiment with making some kind of harness to hang beneath the kennel in order to be certain the camera remained horizontal and pointing in the right direction. If the weather stayed as it was there shouldn't be any problem. If it changed, as it often did in the mountains, suddenly and without warning . . .

Mrs. Cosgrove followed him into the bathroom. She looked skeptical. "Do you think it will ever fly?"

Monsieur Pamplemousse gave a noncommittal shrug. "They asked the same question of the Montgolfier brothers when they set off from the Champ de Mars in 1783." He spoke with more conviction than he actually felt. At least the Montgolfier balloon had been spherical. Aerodynamically, Pommes Frites's kennel left a lot to be desired; it was hardly in the forefront of design.

"And this evening?"

"This evening I shall be even busier." He would need to make a few trial runs with Pommes Frites so that he would get used to the idea of having a miniature *dirigeable* attached to his collar. He might not take kindly to the idea. Both that and testing the helium-filled kennel would have to wait until after dark. And it would have to work first time; in all probability he wouldn't get a second chance.

Aware that Mrs. Cosgrove was looking deflated again, he turned to her. "Perhaps," he said gently, "if you were to help, I might get it all done in half the time. And then . . ."

"And then?" She put down her carrier bag.

"In France there is a saying: '*On s'abandonne à son imagination,*' one lets one's imagination run away with one."

"In England," said Mrs. Cosgrove firmly, "we say that too. We also have one which says: 'There is no time like the present'."

As something soft and silky landed on the bathroom floor there came a sigh of contentment from the other room. Pommes Frites wasn't given to boasting or to blowing his own trumpet, but it was nice to know that his efforts at restoring his master's equilibrium hadn't been entirely wasted.

It was dark by the time Monsieur Pamplemousse followed Pommes Frites out through his bedroom window.

"Good luck!" Mrs. Cosgrove's voice came through the

darkness, muffled by the bulk of the newly inflated kennel as she struggled to push it after them.

"Merci." Privately Monsieur Pamplemousse suddenly realized he was going to need it. Or rather, Pommes Frites would need it.

A feeling of guilt came over him as he clipped the end of the line onto the harness and the makeshift balloon rose into the air. Somewhere along the way his calculations must have gone sadly wrong. Perhaps in his ignorance he had grossly underestimated the lifting power of helium. Whatever the reason, he undoubtedly had a problem on his hands.

If only he'd given it a trial run as planned. Instead of which, his good intentions had gone for nothing, sacrificed in favor of the more immediate desires of the flesh.

Paying out the line centimeter by centimeter, he watched anxiously as the kennel buffeted to and fro against the side of the building.

Merde! If the camera broke one of the windows *en route* the game would be up and no mistake.

At his last medical Pommes Frites had weighed in at around fifty kilograms, but from the feel of things he was going to need every gram. The light breeze he'd noticed earlier in the day had freshened and was full of unpredictable upward currents. For a moment or two he toyed with the idea of adding some extra ballast, then dismissed the thought. Getting the weight exactly right would take time, and now that he'd set the wheels in motion speed was of the essence.

That Pommes Frites was beginning to share his master's anxiety was patently obvious as the end of the line was reached and he began to take the strain. There was a certain lightness to his tread as he set off along the side of the building, a lightness that caused him to gaze skyward more than once as Monsieur Pamplemousse guided him toward his starting position. Much of the time it was hard to tell what thoughts passed through Pommes Frites's mind—he could, if he chose, be very poker-faced—but for once it was patently obvious. He looked decidedly apprehensive.

"Avancez!" Taking advantage of a moment when the moon was temporarily obscured by a cloud, Monsieur Pamplemousse gave him an encouraging pat.

For a full two minutes their luck held. Like a jumbo jet piloted by an inexperienced captain badly in need of a refresher course and using every inch of the runway, Pommes Frites set off, following an unsteady path toward the far end of the building.

Monsieur Pamplemousse held his breath. At least one of his calculations was correct. It was hard to tell from where he was looking, but the camera appeared to be almost exactly in line with the center of the windows. He triggered off the automatic film advance mechanism with the button on the control unit, then began counting the seconds in double rather than single figures in order to keep an accurate time check. One minute, twelve seconds later they were halfway along the side of the building. He glanced down at the control unit. The luminous display showed the figure 18. He breathed a sigh of relief. It meant his allowance of four seconds between shots had been right too.

It was as they neared the end of the building that things began to go wrong. For some reason the camera looked higher than it had at the beginning, rather too near the top of the windows for his liking. Perhaps it was that the ground sloped upward? He looked down again and saw to his horror that the worst had happened. Pommes Frites was treading air; his front paws had already left the ground and their opposite numbers at the rear were about to follow suit.

Monsieur Pamplemousse made a frantic dive forward, only to pull himself up in the nick of time as he realized he was tottering on the edge of a rocky precipice. In any case he had left it too late. Carrying the analogy with a jumbo jet to its ultimate conclusion, Pommes Frites had completed his takeoff.

Bereft of navigational lights, silhouetted in the ghostly light from the moon, now reemerged from behind the cloud, it would under other circumstances have been an awesome sight. Any local inhabitant witnessing the event while staggering home after an evening out with the boys, might well have been excused had he crossed himself and taken an immediate header off the cliffs into the valley far below. As it was, Monsieur Pamplemousse could only stand helplessly by and watch as his friend and mentor executed a steep turn to starboard and then, gaining height with every passing second, set off slowly and ponderously in the direction of the Pyrénées-Orientales.

9

A Developing Situation

It was well after midnight before Monsieur Pamplemousse finally got back to his room.

"Aristide!" Mrs. Cosgrove reached out to help him over the sill. "Are you all right? You've been so long I was beginning to think the worst. How did it all go?"

She felt cold to the touch and he realized she'd probably been waiting by the open window ever since they left. He gave her a quick hug as she drew the curtains. "I shall know for certain when we have processed the film."

"But what happened?" They both blinked as she turned on the light. "You look as if you've been pulled through a hedge backward."

He glanced at his reflection in the mirror. It was an apposite description. All it needed was the word "tree" to be substituted for "hedge" to be true.

"Pommes Frites had an unfortunate accident. Through no fault of his own he became airborne and it was nearly the last we saw of each other. Fortunately I was still holding the control box, so I managed to pull him back safely with the cable. It was, so to speak, his umbilical cord. If that hadn't held —*alors . . . !*" He left the rest to her imagination. It didn't bear thinking about. Full marks to Leitz for quality workmanship. If the cable had been the product of a lesser manufacturer Heaven alone knew what might have happened.

"Poor chap." Mrs. Cosgrove was rewarded by a grateful wagging of the tail as she bent down to give Pommes Frites a pat. "Thank goodness you're safe."

"I'm afraid we lost his kennel in the process. It suffered a puncture when it hit a tree."

Monsieur Pamplemousse spoke as though the whole thing was an everyday happening, but in reality it had been a terrifying experience, seeing Pommes Frites sail off into the night. He would never have forgiven himself had the worst occurred. Climbing the tree in the dark had been nothing by comparison, although getting his precious cargo down in one piece had been another matter; the memory would probably keep him awake at night for some time to come. In the meantime there was work to be done.

"Is everything ready?"

"Just about. I've mixed the chemicals and tried to keep the solutions as near thirty-eight degrees as possible. I stood the jugs in a bowl of water and used your portable coffee heater like you said."

"Good." Monsieur Pamplemousse gave her another appreciative hug. "I don't know what I would have done without you."

As he rewound the film onto its spool he quickly checked the camera. It had survived its emergency landing with hardly a scratch. The settings were all as he had left them. The film safely back in its spool, he clicked open the back of the camera to remove it. Now for the big moment. It was a long time since he'd last done any processing. To ruin things now through some idiotic mistake would be too galling for words.

153

In the bathroom with the lights out, feeling his way around in the pitch dark, he was acutely aware of Mrs. Cosgrove's presence.

The film loaded into its lightproof tank, he reached for the switch. Ten minutes alone in the dark with Mrs. Cosgrove would not be conducive to good darkroom practice. He could also hear Pommes Frites sniffing along the bottom of the door.

"Do you *have* to go back to Paris tonight?"

He shrugged, trying to concentrate on what he was doing and keep an eye on the time as well. "It depends on what's here. If my suspicions are correct then the answer has to be 'yes.' There is a train leaving Carcassonne at four thirty-three in the morning. It gets to Paris in the early afternoon."

"I'll drive you there."

"You don't have to. I can leave the car at the station and make arrangements to have it picked up when I get back to Paris."

"Please. I would like to."

"In that case I would like it too." He couldn't deny it would be very pleasant. The thought of driving through the night in a strange car while trying to map-read at the same time over perhaps two hundred and fifty kilometers or more of mostly winding mountain roads didn't exactly fill him full of joy. Pommes Frites would be fast asleep in the back and he wasn't too sure of his own ability to stay awake.

At exactly twelve seconds before the first five minutes was up he began pouring the developer away, then quickly added the bleach-fix from another jug. Mrs. Cosgrove had done her job well.

After another five minutes he emptied out the second solution and turned on the tap over the basin. Three minutes' wash in cold water should be sufficient; four to be on the safe side.

"Will you be back?"

"It is possible." Even as he spoke the words he knew he wouldn't be. And like the old joke, he knew that she knew that he knew he wouldn't be. To return would imply all kinds of things from which there might be no turning back.

"Who knows? It is a small world." He turned off the tap and began unscrewing the lid of the tank. "Did you bring the hairdryer?"

"It is in the other room." She opened the door and went into the bedroom. Pommes Frites wagged his tail doubtfully.

Monsieur Pamplemousse held the film horizontally between his outstretched hands, keeping a watchful eye on it in case the dryer came too close. In a matter of moments all traces of wetness had disappeared.

Allowing it to spring back into a rough coil, he held the leader over a piece of white paper on the table beneath the overhead light and began pulling it through his fingers, examining it frame by frame.

The first was half wall, half window. Nothing appeared to be happening behind the latter. The second and third frames were of some kind of lounge area. There were a number of figures, mostly male, sitting or standing around in small groups, all so small as to be unrecognizable without being blown up. It looked as though there was a party in progress.

There was another shot of the tower wall. Pommes Frites must have changed his pace slightly. Momentarily diverted, perhaps, by an interesting scent *en route,* or an unexpected cross wind.

The next two or three were much more rewarding. Pin-sharp and brightly lit, they showed a gymnasium, not dissimilar to the one he'd been in on his first day, full of the kind of equipment one would expect in a place where no expense was spared: parallel bars, rowing machines, weight-reducing vibratory belts, racks of dumbbells. The sole occupant was an elderly woman in a track suit who was hard at work on a cycling machine, shoulders hunched, head low down until her close-cropped hair almost touched the dial attached to the handlebars. There was something vaguely familiar about her, but without the aid of a light box or some means of reversing the image it was hard to say exactly what.

Eight and nine were again of the wall. Ten to fourteen were of individual apartments. The main lights must have been out, for they were underexposed and it was hard to tell what was going on.

Frames fifteen to twenty were again well lit. Clearly they showed a kitchen area; white cupboards lined the walls and in the background there was what appeared to be a row of stainless steel ovens. One picture showed some out-of-focus scales in close-up—they must have been standing by the window; another, a row of bowls clearly containing flour. Nearby was a pile of *saucissons*. Number nineteen showed Furze, for once minus his clipboard. He was standing in front of a second set of scales peering at a dial. From number twenty on the film was meaningless, recording for posterity Pommes Frites's journey into space. They might well yield some interesting enlargements, unique in their way, but for the moment Monsieur Pamplemousse had seen enough.

"The answer to your earlier question is 'yes.' I must catch the first train to Paris."

"What time do you want to leave?"

"As soon as possible." He suddenly wanted to get away from Château Morgue. Sensing her disappointment, he tried to console her. "Look, I don't want to leave. I *have* to leave."

It was hard to believe that his expedition with Pommes Frites had gone entirely unnoticed, and if they had been seen word would undoubtedly filter back. There was no time to lose. "But first there are things I must do."

156

"Can I help?"

He took her arm. "I will pack my belongings and then you can help by taking them to the car. Pommes Frites and I will join you there. When we leave we must do it quietly and quickly."

Mrs. Cosgrove looked at him thoughtfully. Almost as if she was seeing him for the first time.

"Are you angry about something?"

"Angry?" Monsieur Pamplemousse considered the remark. Yes, he was angry. He always felt angry when he came across an injustice being done, especially when it involved the very young or those who were too old or too tired to defend themselves. In his days with the Sûreté it had been both a strength and a weakness, but he was glad his feelings had never been blunted. He attempted with difficulty to put it into words.

Mrs. Cosgrove looked relieved as she listened to him. "I thought perhaps it was something I'd said."

Monsieur Pamplemousse took hold of her hand. It felt instantly responsive and yet at the same time it was that of a stranger, making him aware that despite everything they hardly knew each other.

"I don't think that would be possible." He allowed a suitable length of time to elapse before returning to business. "There is one other thing you can do."

"Tell me."

"When Pommes Frites and I leave I want you to go along the corridor to the right. Around the first corner you will find a fire alarm. At the exact time I give you I want you to break the glass. It will clear the building of unwanted people and it will give you an opportunity to leave with the luggage."

"No questions?"

"No questions." The fact of the matter was he didn't as yet have a clear picture of what he intended to do, only the vague outline. He would play it by ear. Events would shape themselves.

Carcassonne station was unrelievedly gloomy and deserted when they arrived. A few faces stared at them uninterestedly through the windows of the waiting train.

Apart from one wrong turn crossing the Massif du Canigou, the drive had been uneventful, but the short cut through Molitg-les-Bains via the D84 had been a disaster, adding perhaps an hour to the journey. In cutting one large corner off the map they had added countless smaller ones, with the result that instead of having plenty of time to spare there was a bare ten minutes before the train was due to leave for Toulouse. Perhaps it was just as well. He didn't like prolonged goodbyes.

"You will have a long journey back."

"That's all right. I don't mind the early mornings—once I'm up." Mrs. Cosgrove glanced skyward. "I shall see the sun rise. I might stop on the way and watch it."

It was true. There wasn't a cloud in sight. It was the time of day he liked best and he almost envied her the drive across the mountains. There would be all manner of wildlife at the side of the road, looking startled as they were caught in the headlights, or shooting off in a panic. And peasants out with guns. They, too, would look affronted by the intrusion of their privacy.

He wondered what was happening back at Château Morgue. Soon after they left a fire engine passed them on its way up, followed by an ambulance and several police cars. He'd caught sight of Inspector Chambard in one of them. It looked as though they were going prepared for some kind of siege. A little later there had been another fire engine, this time with a turret ladder so large the driver was having difficulty negotiating some of the bends. They would need it if they wanted to enter the Tower Block. By the time he'd finished with the lift it would take a skilled electrician several hours to get it going again. The occupants of the Tower Block were well and truly trapped. The only other way down he'd managed to find was an emergency staircase, which came out into the underground garage. He'd rendered that equally *hors de combat.* Sophisticated locks serve a very useful purpose if you want to keep people from making an unauthorized entry, but given a little knowledge they can be made equally effective in keeping others imprisoned.

"I expect your wife will be pleased to see you."

He gave a start. It was the first time she had spoken of Doucette. "How did you know?"

"You don't have to be a detective. You seem very well looked after. Sort of complete. Everything nicely ironed and no loose buttons."

"Anyway, it won't be long before you see George again." It was the first time he'd spoken his name out loud too. He hesitated, unsure of how to say what he wanted to say.

"I'm sorry it had to end like this. I'm sure he'll make up for it." George would be raring to go. Deprived of his *"verts"* for so long there would be no holding him.

Mrs. Cosgrove gave a wry smile. "I should be so lucky. Poor old George. He isn't a bit like that really. Never has been. To tell you the truth, he likes dressing up best." The words came out in a rush, as if she wanted to get them over and done with.

"Dressing up?"

"You know, women's clothing and all that sort of thing. He's got a better wardrobe than I have. Can't help it, poor dear—especially when there's a full moon. That's why I'm here. He had a bit of bad luck in Knightsbridge a few months ago—near the barracks. His case comes up tomorrow and he didn't want to embarrass me."

"A few *months.* That's a long time to wait."

"Three and a half to be exact. He elected to go for trial by jury. That delayed things a bit."

"I trust he has a good lawyer?"

"The best. An old friend." It was her turn to hesitate. "I haven't . . . you know . . . for quite a few years now. Well, fifteen actually."

"Fifteen years!"

For some reason a quotation from Tolstoy flashed through his mind. "Man survives earthquakes, epidemics, the horrors of war, and all the agonies of the soul, but the tragedy that has always tormented him, and always will, is the tragedy of the bedroom." He thought of all the "Georges" he'd arrested in his time, for no better reason than that they were dressed unconventionally as members of the opposite sex. He suddenly felt very sorry for George, that gray figure in the photograph. To be married to Mrs. Cosgrove, and yet . . . *Mon Dieu*! Such waste! And what of her? He wondered if she had always gone in for exotic underwear—just in case. Perhaps she made do with George's cast-offs.

"That is terrible."

"I know. But there you are. They say that what you've never had you don't miss. Perhaps you and I weren't meant. Still," she lowered her eyes, "the little we had was nice. There I go, using that dreadful word again. It wasn't just 'nice'; it was *wonderful*!" She glanced up suddenly and pressed her lips against his.

The station clock showed a minute to go. In less than a minute there would be a hiss and the doors would close automatically. Ever since train drivers had had deductions made from their statutory bonus for every minute they were late arriving they had made sure they left on time.

He hesitated. There would be other trains, other days. What was so special about catching one at 4:33 in the morning? As he took Mrs. Cosgrove in his arms and felt the warmth of her cheek against his, he caught Pommes Frites's eye. Pommes Frites didn't exactly shake his head, but his look said it all.

He was right, of course. There was no going back. Wheels had been set in motion. There would be questions to answer, forms to fill in. He would have to justify his expenses at the *pharmacie* on a P39. Despite having *carte blanche* from the director, Madame Grante would not be at all sympathetic. It would take a lot of explaining.

As the train pulled out and Mrs. Cosgrove became a lone dot on the platform he settled back in his seat and closed his eyes. He pictured her in his mind's eye stopping somewhere on the way back to Château Morgue to watch the sunrise. It was always worse for the one who was left behind. The thought of her loneliness filled him with sadness.

Perhaps he would telephone her when he got back. It would be against the rules, but at least it would let her know that he was still thinking of her; that she wasn't just a ship that had passed in the night.

He would have to think up a good reason. Something innocuous . . . something. . . . Already a corner of his mind was thinking ahead, trying at the same time to fight off a drowsiness brought on by the motion of the train and the warmth of the carriage. The sooner he marshalled his thoughts and got down to the task of writing his report the better. At least on the journey back he wouldn't be bothered by Ananas. Nor would he have to act out the charade of being blind.

He looked down at Pommes Frites. Pommes Frites had no such problems. He was already curled up on the floor and fast asleep. It must be nice being a dog and not having to justify everything you did.

10

The Men from the Ministry

"Entrez!"

Monsieur Pamplemousse used the brief moment between knocking on the door of the director's office and responding to the command by taking a deep mental breath. He had totally lost track of time since his last visit. In some respects it felt like only yesterday, in other ways it could have been weeks or even months. By his side, Pommes Frites, clearly sensible to the importance of the occasion, peered at his reflection in a full-length mirror hanging in the outer office. He seemed reasonably satisfied by what he saw.

Normally, although Pommes Frites's existence was accepted (there had even been talk at one time of giving him his own P39s, but this had been quashed by Madame Grante) his visits to the office of *Le Guide* were restricted to the typing pool on the ground floor. It was a long time since he'd been invited up to the holy of holies.

"Entrez!" The voice was louder this time, and slightly impatient. It coincided with his opening the door.

"Pamplemousse! Welcome back." The director came

around to the front of his desk, arms outstretched in welcome.

For one dreadful moment Monsieur Pamplemousse thought he was about to be embraced. He hoped his momentary recoil had passed unnoticed.

"And Pommes Frites."

The director covered their mutual embarrassment by bending down to administer a pat. Pommes Frites looked even more surprised than his master. Such a thing had never happened before. He responded by jumping up and putting his paws on the director's shoulders.

"Ah, yes. *Bon chien.*" The director removed a handkerchief from his top pocket and dabbed at his face. Pommes Frites's tongue was large and rather wet.

"Gentlemen . . ." He turned and Monsieur Pamplemousse suddenly realized they were not alone. Sitting beneath the portrait of Hippolyte Duval were two anonymous-looking men, immaculately clad in Identikit dark blue suits and matching ties. There was a third figure sitting to one side and slightly behind them. To his surprise he saw it was Inspector Chambard.

He wished now he had put on a suit or worn a jacket rather than a polo-necked jersey. The invitation had sounded informal, come as you are—a kind of end-of-term get-together with the headmaster. Obviously there was more to it than that.

"Gentlemen, Monsieur Pamplemousse and Pommes Frites." The director motioned him forward. "Inspector Chambard I think you have already met. These two gentlemen are from the *Ministère.*"

Monsieur Pamplemousse took due note of the fact that neither the Ministry nor its representatives were mentioned by name.

The taller of the two men rose to greet him. "Monsieur Pamplemousse, we have come to offer our congratulations.

We have received a copy of your report and I can only describe it as a minor masterpiece."

Monsieur Pamplemousse tried hard to conceal his surprise. "It is nothing. I merely put down the facts as I saw them."

"You are too modest." The second of the two men joined his colleague. "Facts, yes. It is what you did with them that matters."

"A *tour de force.*"

"Brilliantly simple."

"Fantastic, yet not impossible."

The dialogue came out so smoothly Monsieur Pamplemousse found himself wondering if they had spent the morning rehearsing it. Perhaps whichever Ministry it was they worked for employed them as a roving double act.

"Tell me, Pamplemousse," the director was not going to be outdone in his own office, "have you ever considered taking up writing for a living? We would hate to lose you, but clearly you have a flair for plot construction. I must confess it is something that has escaped me in the past when reading your culinary reports. They are always very elegant, of course, not to say mouthwatering on occasions, but often bordering on the verbose—like some of your articles in the staff magazine. However, this . . ." He sat down behind his desk and picked up what Monsieur Pamplemousse recognized as a copy of his report. Attached by means of an outsize paperclip were some blow-ups taken from the roll of film he'd left at the same time. "This—"

"Could be your greatest work of fiction," broke in the first of the two men, taking up the running again. He seemed slightly put out by the interruption. "I shall always treasure the picture you conjure up of Château Morgue. Those little old ladies pedaling away like mad on their cycling machines." He broke into a chuckle. "The notion of them all developing outsize calves as a result was a master stroke."

"And the tea parties beforehand. We mustn't forget the tea parties." His companion allowed himself a smile too. "The mountains of *pâtisserie* they consumed—all fresh from the bakery in the Tower Block."

"And for what?"

"So that their heart conditions would be exacerbated to such an extent that violent exercise immediately afterward would bring about an early death—"

"Having, of course, first rewritten their wills in favor of the Schmucks. We mustn't forget that."

"Ici Paris will have a field day."

Monsieur Pamplemousse gazed around the room. The reception being accorded to his report wasn't at all what he had expected. He listened with growing irritation to the peals of uncontrolled laughter.

"Tell me, Pamplemousse," the director wiped his eyes in an effort to restore calm. "What gave you the idea? You have the happy knack of making it sound as though you believe every word you have written."

Feeling somewhat out of his depth, Monsieur Pamplemousse decided to play for time. He said nothing.

The director misinterpreted his silence. "Gentlemen, if I may say so, that is typical of the man. Modest to a fault."

He crossed to a cupboard and withdrew a set of keys from his hip pocket. As he unlocked and opened the door a light came on to reveal a collection of bottles. "I think this calls for a little celebration. Aristide, you set the ball rolling. What will you have?"

Reaching inside the cupboard he opened another door at the back. A second light came on, reflected this time by a frosty interior. "This may interest you—a Malvoisie. It comes from a small grower in the Loire. The last of a dying breed. When he goes I doubt if anyone else will make it."

Monsieur Pamplemousse accepted with alacrity. Apart from providing a welcome change of subject, he was looking forward to the experience. He had come across fleeting

165

references to it in books. Made from the same grape variety as Tokay, its history dated back to the days when the trade routes of Asia Minor all passed through Malvasia. The fact that someone was still making it in the Loire was a discovery indeed.

He held his glass up to the light. The color was pale and strawlike, the flavor on the nose sweet but not cloying, with just a hint of complexity. Altogether a delicious interlude and one which drew murmurs of appreciation all around the room. *Le Guide,* he was pleased to see, was upholding its reputation.

Tongues loosened, a common bond established, the director refilled the glasses and returned to his desk.

"You think the press will buy Pamplemousse's story?"

"If we point them in the right direction. The press will buy anything if it sells more copies. Besides, in a perverse kind of way it is too farfetched for them not to." The leader of the two men turned to his companion for confirmation.

"I agree. And if the newspapers swallow it, then so will the public. There's nothing they like better than a good, juicy scandal."

"The truth is somewhat more prosaic."

"It must not go beyond these four walls."

"Certain people are involved."

"Members of the 'International Set' . . . Ministers . . ."

"Governments could fall."

"Those involved will be punished, of course, but in a roundabout way. They will quietly disappear from the public eye. There will be a number of 'early retirements' around the world. A few 'golden handshakes.' It is better that way."

"Others will be leaned on. They will find life that much more difficult from now on. Some will disappear from the television screens for a while." It sounded like a passing reference to Ananas. Really, the whole thing was too tantalizing for words.

Inspector Chambard reached for his wallet and took out a card. "I must say you kept us on our toes one way and another."

Monsieur Pamplemousse gave a start as he recognized his postcard to Doucette. No wonder she had complained about not receiving one. And to think he had blamed the office of the *Postes et Télécommunications*.

"We knew straight away that it must contain a hidden message of some kind, but you have no idea how long it took us to find it. The expression *'cous-cous'* had us fooled for quite a while."

"It is what I sometimes call my wife," said Monsieur Pamplemousse defensively. "It is a term of endearment I use when we are apart."

"So we discovered . . . in the end!" Inspector Chambard sounded reproachful.

"We had our best men working on it. They tried all the usual things. The message-under-the-stamp routine—the fact that it was on upside down bothered them. They even tried the old invisible-ink-out-of-milk ploy. And there it was —staring us in the face all the time." He turned the card over and held it up for the others to see. "A cross marking 'my floor'—the floor where it was all happening—and the words 'wish you were here.' It was a good thing we'd been warned, though. We had the biggest turntable ladder the Narbonne *Corps de Sapeurs-Pompiers* could provide, well able to reach up to the roof."

"The simplest ideas are always the best in the long run, eh, Aristide?" Basking in the reflection of his subordinate's glory, the director rose and crossed to the cupboard again.

"Communication was the big problem." Inspector Chambard turned to the other two as he held out his glass. "We had been told to stand by but not to interfere; to await orders. We had our man in there—posing as a chauffeur. But I don't mind telling you, when we lost him I was worried."

"The chauffeur?" Monsieur Pamplemousse found himself clutching at straws of information. "You have lost him?"

"He was involved in an accident on the N9. The man is a fool. It seems he hit a sudden patch of sunlight, put on some dark glasses he'd found in the back of the car, and drove straight into a tree."

"He wasn't . . ."

"No. He will be out of the hospital in a couple of weeks —which is more than you can say of the car."

"Your photographs proved most valuable." It was back to the man from the Ministry again. "Take this one . . . *Pardon, Monsieur.*" He reached across and took one of the enlargements from the pile on the director's desk. "What you so delightfully refer to as the kitchen is in reality Doctor Furze's laboratory. At a rough guess—and you probably know more about these things than I do—there must be over one hundred pounds of cocaine in each bowl."

"An on-the-street value of around seventy million francs."

"Grown in Colombia."

"Brought in through Spain and across the Pyrénées."

"Distributed to the larger centers in Paris and Marseilles via the coffins."

"Delivered to the smaller markets inside hollowed-out *saucisses* and *saucissons.*"

"Whenever the time was ripe for a major arrival or distribution there was a convenient death at Château Morgue."

"Madame Schmuck would go into her routine. She was well equipped for it."

"She was born of a Spanish father and an Italian mother."

"They were both mime artists in a traveling theater in

Russia, she found herself on the stage from the word go. Old ladies were her specialty—even as a teenager."

"A change of clothes, a new set of colored contact lenses, a different wig. It was right up her street."

"She would arrive at the Château, expire at a convenient moment, and the wheels would begin to turn. The 'undertakers' would arrive and take her away. Then she would revert to being Madame Schmuck again."

"No one ever stops a hearse."

"*Pouf!*" Inspector Chambard gave a snort. "To think, the number of times I have saluted that hearse! I have even held up the traffic so that it could get through."

Monsieur Pamplemousse sank back into his chair. The picture was suddenly all too clear. The van he'd seen in the garage on his arrival: it had probably been delivering a fresh batch of *charcuterie* that very evening. No wonder its disappearance had caused such consternation. He paled at the thought of what might have happened had the *saucisses* already been filled with cocaine. Both he and Pommes Frites would have been on a high from which there would have been no return.

He glanced at the other photographs. Blown up to twenty-five by twenty, it was easy to see the likeness between Frau Schmuck and the woman he'd first met in his room, and again on the stretcher. Except that was being wise after the event. It was amazing the difference a wig and a pair of colored contact lenses could make. No wonder they'd all had thick calves—that was one thing she couldn't change.

"The other worrying thing about it was the fact that not only had Château Morgue developed into one of the biggest drug centers we've encountered for a long time—it was rapidly becoming a major threat to Western security."

"What started in a small way—the issuing of invitations to a few close friends—grew out of all proportion. Some very powerful people began using the Château, and not just for drugs either. Other perversions started being catered for. Herr Schmuck learned his trade after the war when Germany was in ruins and people would do anything to scratch a living."

"His wife, Irma, was a more than willing assistant."

"The KGB got to hear about it and began making offers to the Schmucks they couldn't refuse. There were fears of blackmail."

The director stirred in his seat. Determined to make his presence felt, he broke into the duologue and took the photographs back. "Two things puzzle me, Pamplemousse. The first is, how did you manage to obtain these? I gather they show rooms on the uppermost floor, and yet clearly they were taken from outside—through the windows. If you had recourse to the hiring of a helicopter, I fear trouble with Madame Grante. We shall need to prepare the ground carefully before we approach her."

"If you will forgive me, *Monsieur le directeur*," Chambard butted in. "There are some matters best left unexplained. I am sure you will understand me if I use the word *sécurité. Sécurité Nationale*."

"As for the cost," the senior of the two officials raised a beautifully manicured hand, "rest assured it will be taken care of."

The director looked suitably impressed. "Of course. I understand. However, that leads me to the second matter." As he spoke he swiveled his chair so that it faced toward the other end of the room.

Monsieur Pamplemousse followed suit and as he did so his gaze alighted first on the model of the Ideal Inspector, clean-shaven, not a hair on his head out of place, immaculately knotted tie. He gave a start as his eyes traveled downward. Sitting on a large sheet of brown paper, mud-stained and somewhat the worse for wear, rather like a captured enemy tank, stood an all too familiar object. It was held down by some large iron stage weights.

Pommes Frites saw it too. He bounded across the room, went round it several times, nearly knocking Alphonse over in the process, before finally giving vent to a loud howl as he settled down in bewilderment in order to consider the problem.

Monsieur Pamplemousse took a deep breath. "It is a difficult matter to explain, *Monsieur*. That is, or rather was, Pommes Frites's kennel—"

"I *know* it is Pommes Frites's kennel, Pamplemousse." The director assumed his Patience Personified voice. "The question is, why is the entrance sealed, and why does it have a quantity of ladies' lingerie glued to the outside? *Black lingerie*. If it is like that on the outside, heaven alone knows what it is like within. The whole thing is totally beyond my comprehension."

Monsieur Pamplemousse felt tempted to say that quite possibly the director might find the remains of some *charcuterie*, but before he had a chance to speak Inspector Chambard took over again.

"We think we know who is responsible, *Monsieur*. It is the work of a certain person in the entertainment world who bears, if I may say so," he inclined his head toward Monsieur Pamplemousse, "a striking physical resemblance to a member of your staff. He is a person of somewhat bizarre tastes and as such he is not welcome in our part of the world. He was last seen by one of the attendants at Château Morgue carrying that object into the bushes on the night of the raid. On that evidence alone we cannot prosecute. Nevertheless, it is not something he would wish to have made public. He has been told in no uncertain terms that should he ever show his face anywhere near Narbonne again we shall *jeter le livre* at him."

The director gazed with distaste at the object under discussion. He gave a sigh. "We live in a sordid world. I sometimes wonder if there is any limit to man's depravity. I wouldn't have your job for all the *thé de la Chine*, Chambard. What on earth would anyone want with an inflatable dog kennel to which items of ladies' underwear have been glued? What would they do with it?''

Inspector Chambard gave a shrug which said it all. He turned to Monsieur Pamplemousse. "With your permission, *Monsieur,* we would like to put it on permanent display in the *Musée des Collections Historiques de la Préfecture de Police* —in the *Déviations Sexuelles* division. Naturally we would pay for the cost of a replacement.''

Monsieur Pamplemousse had been about to protest, but he rapidly changed his mind. Restoring the kennel to its normally pristine condition would not be easy. He'd had to make a slit in the outer inflation tube in order to fill the inside with gas; traces of *lingerie* might be left. Besides, it would be nice to think of Pommes Frites having a place in the Hall of Fame. He might even take him to see it one day. All that apart, he'd caught Chambard's wink.

"Good. That's settled then.'' The senior of the two men from the Ministry stood and drained his glass. His companion followed suit.

"You have rendered an incalculable service to your country, Monsieur Pamplemousse. Not just in the matter of drugs, which is a constant and never-ending battle—as fast as one hole is plugged another opens up—but in an area that affects us all: the security of the western world. There will be a decoration, of course.''

"In the fullness of time. It wouldn't do to arouse too much interest for the time being.''

"Pommes Frites, too. We understand it was he who located the *charcuterie.''*

At the mention of his name, coupled with the evocative word *"charcuterie,''* Pommes Frites pricked up his ears. As far as he was concerned there had been a great deal of talk and very little action. He was also getting hungry. Perhaps things were about to take a turn for the better.

Monsieur Pamplemousse hesitated. Doucette would be

pleased, but deep down he knew he couldn't possibly accept. It was easier for him; he could evaluate the risks involved. Pommes Frites, on the other hand, did things out of love and a generosity of spirit, a simple desire to please his master. He was happy to be rewarded with a kind word and a pat at the end of it all.

"What I did was nothing. At one time it would have been part of my job. However, a mention for Pommes Frites would be nice. Something small he can hang on his collar. I'm sure he would appreciate it."

Behind his back the director raised his shoulders in a shrug which was part exasperation, part pride at Monsieur Pamplemousse's reaction.

Au revoirs said, the men from the Ministry departed; perhaps they had a matinee performance elsewhere. Inspector Chambard nodded and followed them at a discreet distance.

The director motioned Monsieur Pamplemousse and Pommes Frites to remain behind. "There is a *soupçon* of wine left in the bottle. It would be a pity to waste it."

"Merci, Monsieur." As Monsieur Pamplemousse settled down again he glanced across at Pommes Frites's kennel and then with some distaste at Alphonse.

The director read his thoughts. "I think Alphonse will be taking an early retirement," he said. "I have decided that he is, perhaps, a little too perfect for our requirements. To tell you the truth, his smile is beginning to get on my nerves. I have to cover him up from time to time."

"Holier than thou?" ventured Monsieur Pamplemousse.

"Holier than all of us, I fear, Aristide," replied the director. "I think it is high time he went back to the shop window whence he came. He will be just in time for the spring sales. He has served his purpose and it seemed a good ploy at the time.

"As you will have gathered from the letter, I was under some compulsion from the powers that be to send you to Château Morgue. It came about as the result of a chance remark at an official function when I happened to talk of our plans.

"Tell me, Aristide," the director dropped his voice. "These things intrigue me, it is such a different world from the one I am used to. The letter . . . Did you . . . did you eat it?"

Monsieur Pamplemousse lowered his eyes. He couldn't bring himself to tell a direct lie.

The director followed his glance and light dawned. "Pommes Frites again! I should have known. Some kind of emergency, no doubt. I will not embarrass you by probing too deeply."

Draining his glass, he crossed to the cupboard and closed both doors with an air of finality. "Ah, Pamplemousse, I do envy you at times—you people in the field. You lead exciting lives."

Monsieur Pamplemousse took his cue. The interview was at an end.

"No doubt you will be taking Madame Pamplemousse out for a surprise *dîner* tonight. Where is it to be, Robuchon, Taillevant? Let my secretary know and I will have reservations made."

"It is kind of you, Monsieur, but I think we shall be eating *chez nous.*" Doucette would be highly suspicious if he took her to either of the places the director had mentioned. They were reserved for very special occasions. She would think he was suffering from a guilt complex and suspect the worst.

"I understand." As he opened the door the director assumed his man-of-the-world voice for the benefit of anyone who happened to be listening. "We will save it for another time."

As Monsieur Pamplemousse left the director's office and made his way down the corridor, he had an odd feeling in the back of his mind that something was missing; some piece of the jigsaw was still not yet in place. Turning a

174

corner, he found Inspector Chambard waiting for him. They shook hands briefly and fell into step.

"*Déjeuner?*" Chambard eyed him hopefully. "Have it on me. I am not often in Paris."

"Why not? We can take a stroll toward the fourteenth. There is a little *bistro* I know. On Tuesdays they have *co-triade*—we can share one if you like." The Malvoisie had sharpened his appetite for seafood. They could help it on its way with a bottle of Muscadet. Who was it who said the good Lord decreed that there should be fine wine made at the mouth of the Loire to go with the *fruits de mer*?

"The Muscadet they serve is one of the few still made *sur lie*—without racking. It is full of character."

Pommes Frites knew the *bistro* too. He was well known there and often got invited round the back. His pace quickened as he picked up the scent. It was nice to be back in the old routine.

While they were waiting for someone to come and take their order, Inspector Chambard took out his notebook and flipped open the cover. He turned a few pages.

"I hope you will not mind my asking this. You do not have to answer, of course. It is, as it were, a matter between friends. However, I, too, have to write out a report and there are one or two loose ends. You understand?" He gave a wry smile. "I am afraid I do not have your imagination. I have to discover the exact truth."

Monsieur Pamplemousse nodded. He understood. Once a policeman, always a policeman. He wished Chambard would get on with it.

"Firstly, when our man met you in Narbonne you did not respond to the prearranged code message. I assume you had a good reason?"

"Ah, the prearranged code message." Monsieur Pamplemousse found himself playing for time again.

"Our man said 'All is for the best,' and you were meant to say 'in the best of possible worlds.' It is from Voltaire."

"One cannot be too careful," said Monsieur Pamplemousse. "Besides, I am used to working alone."

Inspector Chambard looked hurt. "Our man thought you must be Ananas after all. We'd had word that he was on the same train. I'm afraid he must have given you a rough ride. He does not consider himself one of Ananas's greatest fans."

"He is not alone in that."

The point was taken. "I sympathize. But I think you will be rid of the problem for a while. If our friend knows what is good for him he will be keeping a low profile. To do him justice I don't think he realized what he was letting himself in for. A weak man himself, he was attracted by those of like mind. Such people have extrasensory perception." There was a pause.

"One other thing. Tell me, *was* it you with the English *Madame* the other evening?"

"We had dinner in the village." Monsieur Pamplemousse wondered what was coming now.

"And do I have your word that it was not you who was responsible for the robbery in the ladies' changing rooms?"

"You do."

Inspector Chambard looked relieved. He methodically drew some lines across the page, then snapped the book shut, replacing a rubber band which held the covers together.

"You'd be surprised at the things that go on at a health farm. Cut people off from their food and they get desperate. I have over forty pairs of *culottes* unaccounted for. I can't tell you what a headache that is. The only ones we have retrieved so far are those on Pommes Frites's kennel. But we will find them. Never fear. We will find them."

But Monsieur Pamplemousse was hardly listening. *"Pardon."* He rose from the table. "I have an urgent telephone call to make."

How long had he been in Paris? Three days? He wondered if he had left it too late. His room might have been searched. Worse still, Mrs. Cosgrove could have already gone back to England. As the ringing tone started he found himself crossing his fingers.

"Château Morgue?" At least the switchboard was still operating. "Madame Cosgrove, *s'il vous plaît.*"

"*Oui, Monsieur.*"

He breathed a sigh of relief. She must still be there. Conscious of a couple at a nearby table half listening to his conversation, he turned his back. In a mirror behind the bar he could see a reflection of the kitchen. Pommes Frites was busy with a bowl.

"Anne!"

"*Oui,* I am well, thank you." He felt excited at hearing her voice again. "I am sorry . . . I wanted to telephone, but . . . I wasn't sure if you would still be there." It sounded a feeble excuse.

"Tomorrow? I hope you have a good journey."

"He's got off? You must be relieved—"

"I hope so too."

"Listen . . . before you go, can you do me a favor? Under my bed you will find a parcel. Could you post it for me?"

"No, not *to* me, *for* me." That would be a disaster—if a parcel of assorted *lingerie* arrived while he was away and Doucette opened it by mistake, he would never hear the last of it.

"What address?" He thought for a moment. "Address it to Madame Grante, care of *Le Guide.*" That would give her something to think about. He fed another coin into the slot. "I have only a little time left." One franc's worth to be precise and there were so many things he wanted to say.

"Who knows? One day, perhaps?"

"*Oui,* it is a small world. Listen . . . thank you again, *et bonne chance.* George too."

There was a click and she was gone. The P.T.T. didn't even leave time for an *au revoir.*

He arrived back at the table at the same time as the tureen of *cotriade*. Alongside it was a bowl of the traditional heart-shaped *croûtes*. He wondered if he could distract Chambard's attention long enough to filch one. It would be a reminder of his times with Mrs. Cosgrove.

He glanced out of the window. "It looks as if we may have snow." It was true. There was a bitterly cold wind blowing from the north. People were hurrying by with their coat collars turned up.

He quickly transferred one of the *croûtes* onto his chair seat, holding it in place with his leg.

But his satisfaction was short-lived. As Inspector Chambard turned back he felt something push against him. Almost immediately there was a loud crunching noise from underneath the table.

Pommes Frites looked up at him gratefully. It was good to be back and to have such a thoughtful master, ever sensitive to his needs. The bowl of *navarin d'agneau* the chef had given him had been nice, but it tasted even better when it was followed by a piece of fried bread which had been well rubbed with garlic.

Life, in Pommes Frites's humble opinion, had few better things to offer. And even though he could see that for some reason best known to himself, Monsieur Pamplemousse didn't entirely share his view, instinct told him that it was only a matter of time before he would.